THE MILL FARM
and other stories

by

George Sweeting

Highgate of Beverley
Highgate Publications (Beverley) Limited
2013

DEDICATION
'She hath done what she could' – St Mark Chapter 14, Verse 8
To my dear wife Margaret, our daughters Elizabeth and Helen, my parents and many
others who all have an abundance of heart.

NOTE
Part of the proceeds from the sale of this book will go to the Yorkshire Scan Appeal,
which works so hard to raise funds to support the non-surgical treatment of cancer at
the Hull MRI Centre. Donate or find out more at www.yorkshirescanappeal.co.uk.

ACKNOWLEDGEMENTS
Former course tutors Nora Jones, Vivien Hunter and Judith Atkinson at the University of
Hull Centre for Lifelong Learning; the late Ken Mallinson, Principal Lecturer in English at
the then North Lindsey Technical College; Dr Margaret Sumner for all her unstinting hard
work in bringing this book to completion; Barry Sage and Dr John Markham of Highgate
Publications for all their friendly help; Rob Stanley, formerly Chief Librarian, Kingston
upon Hull City Council.

PERMISSIONS
Innes Photographers for permission to use the photograph of Mill Farm, Etton, which
appears in *Etton – A Village of the East Riding* by Gail M White.

All other photographs, copyright of the author.

British Library Cataloguing in Publication Data.
A catalogue record for this book is available from the British Library.

© 2013 George Sweeting

George Sweeting asserts the moral right to be identified as the author of this work.

ISBN 9781 902645 59 9

Published by
Highgate of Beverley

Highgate Publications (Beverley) Limited
24 Wylies Road, Beverley, HU17 7AP
Telephone (01482) 866826

Produced by
Highgate Print Limited
24 Wylies Road, Beverley, HU17 7AP
Telephone (01482) 866826

CONTENTS

FOREWORD
by
NORA JONES

I first met George in 2001 when he joined one of my creative writing classes at the University of Hull. He had previously taken a course in language and writing skills where his tutor told him 'You must write!' So write he did, and I had the pleasure of reading and guiding George's work for the next six years.

I was impressed by George's evocative sense of place and descriptions of nature in his stories. Later, George developed his characters, and I encouraged him to extend their dialogue, giving them more voice. He quickly did both to great effect.

George, admittedly, is influenced by the writing of Thomas Hardy, D. H. Lawrence and H. E. Bates. With them, he shares a descriptive style and strong sense of place. Also a deep love of the English language: its rhythm, sound, variety and natural flow and this is evident in his work. George's stories have a thread of sadness running through them but many of them end on a note of hope. Both of these elements add to their resonance and poignancy. George also has a great interest in history so it is no surprise that over half of these stories have their setting in an earlier period.

George has already had some of his work published. The short stories, 'The Printer's Devil' and 'They Matter' appeared in the 2002 issues of *The Yorkshire Journal* and 'Just Around the Corner' was in the autumn 2003 edition of the short story magazine *Scribble*. Extracts of George's childhood memories were included in Gervase Phinn's 2008 publication, *All Our Yesterdays*. He also had two stories in the Hird Publications anthologies, 'A New Moon with the Old Moon in Her Arms' in *Liquorice Ice Cream (2006)* and 'The Mill Farm' in *Postcards to Aunty Mag (2008)*.

George was encouraged in his writing by his late wife Margaret, who was privileged to hear the original versions of her favourite stories especially, 'A Bride in the Hand,' 'The Last Tango', 'Elviras' and 'The Mill Farm'. George's fellow students appreciated the finished stories and listened attentively whenever he read them in our selected reading sessions. Amongst my own favourites are 'A New Moon with the Old Moon in her Arms', which vividly evokes the theme of war and highlights George's sensitively drawn characters, 'Wobbly Wood' with its gentle humour and intimate glimpses of childhood, and 'David', a poignant and vividly narrated Christmas story.

I sincerely hope that in publishing this anthology, George will reach the wider audience that his work deserves and that his future readers will enjoy and appreciate his stories as much as I have done over the years.

THE MILL FARM

Rather grandly, it was called Mill Farm, when really it was just a smallholding – an island of vegetables enclosed by low, short-cropped hedges and surrounded by arable land for cereals and pasture for stock. Two brothers were busy cutting cabbages in one of the fields. They paused, raising sunburnt arms to their eyes when a crack of sunlight appreared from behind the gathering clouds.

'I'll have to finish up now,' said Edwin. He looked towards a large Victorian rectory, now a residential home for the elderly. 'I want to wash and change before I go down to Lintern Grange this evening.'

'Mother ill there last year,' said his younger brother Alan, slashing another cabbage from its stalk and throwing it up into a muddy trailer. 'Now Aunt Mary in the same place.' He stuck his machete in the compacted earth and glanced towards the farm. Bricks were loose on the old mill tower; windows were boarded up or empty of glass; traces of green paint dotted their rotting frames.

'There's new girl helping at the Grange,' said Edwin. 'Mary seems to have taken a liking to her.' Edwin had been married, briefly, some twenty years ago, but it was something the brothers never talked about. Susan had been a librarian. With her slender white hands, she'd picked some garden fruit that first summer but never worked in the fields. Then during the long, wet, strangely silent days of November, with their endless drift of low, dark clouds, and the wind as sharp as Edwin's machete, Susan returned to her parents in the city. Edwin accepted her sudden departure with quiet resignation, in his stolid, countrified way.

'I'll go down to the Grange if you want,' said Alan. He knew how much his brother dreaded the thought of making conversation with their elderly, unmarried aunt.

Edwin scratched the greying ginger stubble sprouting unevenly on his leathery face. 'Would you mind?' he said. 'Thanks.'

Back at the outbuildings near the mill, the two brothers unhitched the trailer from the tractor and went their separate ways, Edwin plodding wearily to the new house he had helped to build for his young bride, Alan to the old family farmhouse, where he washed off the day's mud and began to prepare his tea. The sun had dropped behind a small plantation when Alan finally walked down the hill to the village to visit his aunt.

*   *   *   *

'They're over there somewhere, in the drawer,' said Aunt Mary, taking a bony, purple hand from her Zimmer frame and pointing towards the single bed. Her complexion remained fresh, shiny as an apple. 'I'll call for Gina. She'll find them. I can't get used to this place – everything in the same room. I hope you're keeping the house clean.' Tears began to trickle down her cheeks. 'I'd like to come home, but I'm not sure I ever will.'

Alan looked away. A few old black and white studio photographs stood in small frames on the bedside table, and a clean, neatly folded nightgown lay on the chair beside it.

'Still, I'll have to make the best of it. Food's not bad, I suppose. If only I could walk a bit.' Painfully, Aunt Mary lifted her swollen, bandaged leg from a cushioned stool. 'Gina took my bank books into town a couple of days ago to get the interest written up. I want you to know how much I've got in there. Well, it's bound to happen sometime and you'll ...' Her voice dropped to a whisper as a girl came into the room.

'We're trying to find Aunt's bank books,' said Alan, relieved to see a pretty young face.

'They're in the bedside cupboard – bottom drawer, at the back.' Gina had been surprised to see how much the books contained: just over £15,000 when the cashier returned them.

'You should keep these,' she said, handing them to Alan.

Edwin will be pleased, he thought.

Later, in the wide entrance hallway, he tried to prolong his conversation with the girl. Gina's simple white overall hung loosely over a shapely figure. The scent of her perfume, and the suddenness of it, reminded him of long-ago nights at dances in town and awkward attempts to put his arm around a girl's waist. He smiled, remembering also Edwin's clumsy steps on the dance floor.

* * * *

A couple of weeks later Alan and Gina left Lintern Grange together. 'Would you like to come down to the Royal Oak?' he asked, overcoming his shyness.

The next time he saw her, she complained about her accommodation at the home. 'My room's too small,' she said, pointing to a single window in one of the attic turrets. 'I'm always on call. I'm never completely away from work.'

The next month they decided to visit the coast in Alan's van. Gina was still unhappy about living in at Lintern Grange.

'I've rooms empty at the farm now Aunt Mary's in the home,' Alan suggested hopefully.

* * * *

The first clumps of daffodils beside the short farm track were blowing in the blustery wind, and the surrounding fields coming alive with the green shoots of wheat and barley, when Gina moved into Aunt Mary's room facing the old mill tower. Edwin and Alan were planting out beetroot on the day she arrived. They watched her walk over the humpback bridge that crossed the disused railway line running through the farm.

'This Jenny, as you call her, looks a fair bit younger than you,' grumbled Edwin. He was annoyed because his brother hadn't consulted him first. 'I hope you're charging her a fair rent?'

'It's Gina, not Jenny,' said Alan. 'She'll be able to help out with the accounts and the farm sales, when she's not at Lintern Grange.' He paused. Should he go on, he wondered? 'Gina's a strong lass – not like your Susan.'

'No need to bring that up,' said Edwin bitterly, and walked away.

* * * *

The May blossom hung like thousands of eyes along the railway track the day Aunt Mary died. After the funeral, Edwin joined Alan and Gina for the evening meal. No one had come back to the house: some farming relatives from Lincolnshire had attended the service, but they left soon afterwards. Stock to feed, they said.

Edwin thought back to the funeral teas of his childhood: so many fresh-faced country people had jostled for space in this same room as they debated the price of crops or the merits of the latest farm machinery.

2

'What are you doing with that?' said Edwin abruptly, recognising his mother's ring on Gina's finger.

He'd noticed a light shining in his aunt's bedroom for a few nights after the girl's arrival. Now, though, it was always in darkness and the curtains remained undrawn.

'I found it in a drawer,' said Gina, spreading her fingers wide. Alan coloured up and they continued to eat their meal in silence. Eventually Edwin pushed his plate aside and left.

*   *   *   *

A vast, languid silence surrounded the orderly, tilled lines of vegetables as Edwin lingered by the old mill. The evening wind ruffled the dry, wispy heads of barley, paler now in the yellow dusk. The air was heavy with the scent of hawthorn and warm on his bare forearms. A blackbird sang from the top of the mill, its melancholy call echoing over the fields.

He would have to make an effort: he was fond of his younger brother. Gina had a bright face and a light in her eyes. She wasn't slovenly or sulky; nor did she have Aunt Mary's complaining tongue. He knew marriage had made him suspicious of women. He'd try and do better for Alan's sake. But his anger had yet to subside when he turned to go indoors.

*   *   *   *

'I'd like a car,' Gina announced one evening as she cleared away the plates after their meal. 'Just a small one.' Gina knew Aunt Mary's inheritance remained untouched, and she'd seen the size of the cheques from the vegetable wholesaler. Alan, hands thick and red, was counting cash from the farm sales and bagging it up for the bank.

*   *   *   *

'Who's that?' Edwin said to his brother as they cut sprouts later that month. A small car had stopped outside the farmhouse, where Prince, their tired old black labrador, was pushing himself up on his shaky hind legs.

'It's Gina,' mumbled Alan, returning to his work.

'You've bought her a car?' The lines on Edwin's face grew deeper still.

'Yes.' Alan moved on to another row of sprouts.

'What were you thinking of? We need a new van first for the business?'

'It didn't cost much.' The day was dark and misty and Alan's hands cracked and raw as he reached for his flask. Muddy rainwater filled the deep crevices in the hedge bottoms.

'I hope it came out of your share of the money?' said Edwin. 'Anyway Gina should be down here helping us.'

'She's been doing the banking and the accounts.' Alan slashed even harder at the sprouts. 'The accountant's coming this afternoon. Then she's got some ordering to do.'

'And how long will that take her?' Edwin stared coldly at his brother and the rest of the day passed in an edgy silence.

*   *   *   *

Forrester & Jefferson's newest employee knocked softly on the door of Mill Farm.

'Good morning,' he said. 'I'm John Greenwood.'

Gina offered him a drink and a scone. 'Just baked this morning,' she said, wiping traces of flour from the light, downy hairs on her arms. 'Yours must be such an interesting job,' she continued brightly. 'You must be very clever and good with figures.'

'Well, yes.' John blushed, struggling to balance the plate on his knee. He wanted to tell her that he'd just passed an examination. She was older than him, but not by much.

His hands were trembling as he skipped through his file. 'Here, let me take that,' said Gina, putting it on the table. 'Now, what do you need?'

'Bank statements, paying-in books, paid invoices and cheque-book stubs, please.' John rubbed his chin, a little disarmed by the loss of his file.

'I think they're in the car,' said Gina. She rummaged around for her keys. 'Yes, that's it. I won't be long.'

She returned empty handed, shaking her head. 'We're not doing very well, are we? I must have left them at the bank – or was it the hairdresser's?'

She smiled at him, wide eyed. Could she be teasing him?

'Don't worry,' said John. 'I can come again. Do you have the records for your farm sales perhaps? The cash sales – you know, for the produce you sell at the door.'

'I do, but I haven't entered them all up yet,' Gina replied quickly. 'You could look at them when you call back for the statements. You'll need to examine them both together, won't you?'

She passed John his file as he moved towards the door. 'Better not forget this,' she added.

'Everything alright with the accountant?' asked Alan that evening.

'Yes,' said Gina. 'He's got to come back, though.'

Slumped in his chair, Alan was too weary to ask why, and by the time she returned sleep had overtaken him.

*　　*　　*　　*

A week later, the day dawned still under a cloudless dome of blue. In the village below, the strong sunlight even brightened the war memorial with its weathered stone carving of the crucified Christ. By noon, the last of the barley in the neighbouring field was starting to stir. And by dusk, as great swirls of cawing, wind-blown rooks battled to roost in the tree tops, the wind was rustling through the hedges criss-crossing the dark land.

'Stormy night to come,' said Alan, anxious about possible damage to his vegetables. Gina untied her ribbon and gently shook her head so that her long hair fell loosely over her shoulders. She knew it gave him pleasure. Then, illuminated by a single light on the dressing-table, she brushed her hair. She smiled softly to herself, aware that Alan was watching her reflection in the mirror.

'Are you alright?' he asked, listening to the roof tiles grating against each other as they were lifted by the wind. 'Has Edwin been upsetting you? He'll come round one day. You'll see.'

'No, it's not Edwin.'

Alan nodded. Perhaps she'd bought something for the house and wanted to show it to him before his brother had time to be critical.

Downstairs, the grandfather clock chimed as it had for generations. In the cold sitting-room, by the dying firelight, Prince would be settling down for the night.

'There's something I must tell you.' Gina's expression grew serious. 'Something you should know.'

Out in the yard, a door slammed.

'I'll go down and fasten that,' said Alan. He smiled. 'Did I ever tell you the old tale about Mill Farm. If the wind got up during the night – enough to turn the sails – one miller's wife would make her husband go out through the bedroom window and down a ladder. She didn't want him clumping downstairs and waking the entire household!'

'I'm not your wife,' said Gina, 'and the mill has lost its sails.' She looked out at the black stump of the tower and then took her dressing-gown from the back of the bedroom door. 'I'm still half dressed,' she continued tenderly. 'You stay in bed. You must be tired out. We'll talk when I get back.'

'I find it difficult – this living together,' said Alan hesitantly. 'It's something I've never done before.'

'It's what men and women do when they love one another,' Gina replied lightly, with another toss of her hair. 'And you do love me, don't you?'

Alan said nothing. Deep in thought, he watched as she put on her dressing-gown and pulled the cord tight around her waist. Prince gave a muffled bark as she descended the creaking stairs.

*   *   *   *

Outside, Gina shivered in the cold night air. Dampness rose in the yard. The hills, so softly rounded in daylight, appeared immense and unfamiliar – so too the tall beech trees running in lines down to the village below. The strong, gusting wind was flecked with rain. An occasional pulse from the lighthouse on the chalk headland flashed across the coastal plain. Then a crack of thunder set the hounds in the nearby hunt kennels yelping restlessly, and a sudden downpour soaked her.

Gina stumbled across the yard, pulling her dressing-gown more tightly around her. She tripped over some rutted tractor marks that were quickly filling with rainwater. It's the mill door that's open, she thought with a start. Gasping, she struggled to fasten the heavy, rough-edged door back on its hook, crying out in pain as a splinter went into her finger.

Inside the mill lay all the rusty detritus of past generations. She groped beneath some coarse sacking and found the purse she'd hidden. Unclasping it, she removed some notes and ran them through her cold fingers. She didn't want the money, she knew that now. Alan was honest, decent. He'd trusted her. So had Aunt Mary. She thought of the bank statements she'd kept from him. She'd been reckless with their money – a thief. She turned the word slowly over and over in her mind. Perhaps when she returned to their room, he'd forgive her.

She began to put the notes back in the purse, but a blast of wind startled her and they scattered like hawthorn blossom in the darkness. She heard a slow creak outside. Time seemed to hang suspended, and the blood ran cold in her veins. First a few bricks fell. Then the thick centre-post toppled, crashing down in a cloud of dust.

Later, alone in her gentle, see-saw world, came the voices of the brothers. Her hand still gripped the purse. A beam of torchlight picked it out, emerging from the rubble and the branches of a dead tree.

*   *   *   *

Early one March morning, six years later, Alan received two letters. One, he knew, came from Gina. The other was from the wholesaler. Alan ripped it open and found a cheque inside. He smiled at the memory of Edwin's gentle mockery: 'Flowers might bring a better price than vegetables,' had been his brother's comment when Alan first planted a few daffodils around the edge of one of their fields.

Gina's letter was added to the pile behind the mantelpiece clock. Heavy showers were forecast for later that morning, and Alan still had some planting out to do.

When the first drops of rain began to fall, he left his fields and returned to the house. He read and re-read Gina's letter: now was the time to talk to his son. A young girl from the village cared for Harry. Alan could hear their voices now behind the low hawthorn hedge surrounding the garden. He had needed help to bring up the boy, but he knew that their life had been easier because he could start and finish work whenever he wished.

Harry had a healthy flush on his cheeks. He was sitting on a swing and held out his arms for Alan to steady it.

'You can go home if you like, Katherine.' Alan pointed to the rain sheeting down over over the hills. 'I'll look after Harry for the rest of the day.'

They watched as the girl cycled off down the track to the road and eventually disappeared from sight over the humpback railway bridge.

Alan held Harry's hand as they walked toward the site of the mill. 'There was an accident here once,' he said to his son. 'I'm going to show you where it happened.' He took off his cap. 'This is where your Uncle Edwin rescued your mother one stormy night. A tree fell onto the old mill that once stood here.'

Alan stopped to pick up a few loose chippings of red brick.

'Edwin, that's my middle name,' said Harry. The boy was puzzled. 'What was this uncle like?'

Alan stooped to gather a handful of earth. 'This is what your uncle Edwin lived for,' he said.

Edwin had grown even more solitary after the storm. A bit crazy, some thought, when they saw his tractor charging through the village.

Edwin had panicked as they cleared the rubble from Gina's body. Later, however, all Alan could remember was his brother's bitterness: 'Steals your heart, then steals your money,' he'd said, his blue eyes hardening. They returned to their fields in an angry silence deeper than any drift of snow on the Yorkshire Wolds.

Then one day Edwin was gone. Now his house lay as neglected as the old mill used to be.

Gina had blamed herself. Nothing could reach her. She had her injuries to contend with, and then Harry's birth. She returned briefly to Mill Farm on occasion but often disappeared without trace. Now she was in hospital where Alan could at least visit her.

'The doctors say your mother's much better,' said Alan. His face brightened. 'She's ready to come home. Do you remember how sad she was? That's all gone now.'

He placed his hand on Harry's shoulder and they walked back towards the house. On the grassy mound behind them – all that now remained of the mill – a few daffodil spears swayed in the wind. Stunted by the severe winter cold, each spear drooped like the slender, cupped hand of a woman as she holds it out to be kissed.

WOBBLY WOOD

You wouldn't think something inanimate could strike such fear into the human heart, well would you? But that's what a piece of wood did to me, every Wednesday afternoon, all those years ago.

It was an uneven contest from the start. Frank Broom used his armoury of tools – mallets, saws, drills, chisels, planes and hammers – to make objects that filled him with pride. But in my inept hands the results were very different.

Frank had built his little empire next to the main woodwork room. Far removed from the rest of the school, with armchair, kettle, toaster, gas hob and a small wireless for the racing results, it was better equipped than a seaside B&B. Rumour had it there was even a bottle of whisky hidden beneath the knitted tea cosy.

Waiting outside on rainy afternoons before we trooped in for our woodwork lesson, we could see Frank sitting with his feet up behind the little net curtain. Day in, day out, the same threadbare brown overall clothed his bulky frame, the shiny patches on each elbow seamlessly stitched by Mrs Broom. Frank was never without a pencil stub behind his left ear, taking it out and licking it thoughtfully before making a start on the day's runners and riders. He was also very tight on security. Once a week, he took his great bunch of keys, unlocked the door to the woodwork room door and became my jailer. Then he would smile, thick lips parting to reveal a mouthful of teeth like slanting gravestones. He sported a defiant, jutting chin, fly-away eyebrows badly in need of a trim from some of his tools, and red cauliflower ears, a legacy of his rugby career. When he was annoyed, the colour would spread like an incoming tide from his ears to the rest of his face.

His name was apt – since broom is a woody sort of plant and he taught woodwork. We called him Bristly, no need to explain why, but also because he was always bristling with anger. Our games teacher was called Mr Ball – now there's another coincidence – and one of the language teachers was Mr French. In junior school we had a Miss Bosomworth ... but we'll not go into that now.

Frank loved the grainy smoothness of wood and would run his worker's hand over a plank as if he were caressing his wife. Don't misunderstand me. It's not that I'd anything against wood entirely. The sight of a great tree, full-leaved in spring, swaying in the wind – that was a different matter, far removed from the soulless planks of the woodwork room. I always found the lines of the tall autumn poplars in the cemetery next to the school a wistful sight, fluttering their dry leaves and sounding like the sea when you stood underneath them.

Joints were my biggest headache. No, not my knees and ankles, but those you were meant to chisel out of wood. My efforts never brought two pieces of wood together in that perfect snug union we were aiming for – the dove never tailed, the mortise never slotted into the tenon. Again, fret was an appropriate name for the saw because I snapped so many of those wretched, brittle blades.

Each year the local councillors visited the school and for that one day we were expected to appear bright eyed and enthusiastic – unusual for the pupils of a 1950s secondary modern.

'Slight change of plan,' boomed Bristly one afternoon. He'd received an urgent call from the head at lunchtime and splashes of egg from his fry-up now adorned his brown overall. 'In addition to the visit this year there will be work on display for all our curriculum subjects, woodwork included. I'd like you lot to make either a clothes-horse or a stool.'

I was told to make a stool.

Two Wednesday afternoons later my stool still wobbled. In desperation, I wedged the joints with cigarette cards and bubblegum. It looked quite good, but it was a shame to crumple up my Doris Day cards. I was on the cusp of adolescence and I'd just swapped them for England's wizardly wingers, Stanley Matthews and Tom Finney.

'All your work will be displayed on this raised plinth,' bristled Bristly.

At the end of the lesson he left the room and I placed my stool at the back of the display. You could tell it was mine. Like everything else I made it was smeared with blood. Bristly hadn't inspected it: he was in a flap about the visit and didn't have the time.

'The cream of industrial homes – that's what you are and that's what you will remain when you leave this place of learning,' crowed Alderman Eric Attwood, his narrow shoulders drooping under his heavy gold chains of office. He droned on: 'I can see all the work on display today is of the highest standard.'

'Isn't it lovely?' fluttered Amanda Attwood, the young Lady Mayoress. Rumour had it she'd met her husband on a package tour to Spain. 'Rather hot in here though,' she murmured, unbuttoning the jacket of her tight-fitting chequered costume.

A line of adolescent eyes turned as glassy as playground marbles.

'I really must sit down,' she swooned. 'I'm feeling rather faint.'

We'd been worried that the Lady Mayoress might be overcome during her tour of inspection by the aroma of our craft-room glue or the smelly froth foaming up from the canteen drains, but never by the heat.

'Why not have a nice sit down on one of these stools, dear?' beamed the alderman.

And that's when I noticed someone had moved my stool to the front of the display!

The Lady Mayoress hovered gracefully over a number of stools before eventually choosing to place her well-upholstered bottom on my exhibit. She crossed her shapely legs as if perching at a bar and smiled as if the *Gazette* was taking her photograph.

There was a wobble of wood, a splintering crash and a shriek. The legs of the Lady Mayoress protruded from a tangle of stools and clothes-horses, waving in the air like those of a faller in the Grand National. Bristly jumped in to help but slipped and toppled like one of his planks, landing on top of her. The two bodies wrestled.

Someone who thought whisky just the thing for an emergency had gone to Bristly's room, removed the tea-cosy, and returned with a smeary glass full of honey-coloured liquid. Bristly's face and thick neck were crimson as he and the Lady Mayoress disentangled themselves.

Alderman Attwood cleared his throat in disapproval.

I never had another woodwork lesson. I spent the rest of the summer term helping to prepare the cricket square on Wednesday afternoons. Then I was sent to sweep up the shavings in the woodwork room. Well, I couldn't completely abandon Bristly Broom, could I?

A NEW MOON WITH THE OLD MOON IN HER ARMS

Late, late yestreen I saw the new Moon,
With the old Moon in her arms;
And I fear, I fear, my Master dear!
We shall have a deadly storm.

(*Sir Patrick Spens*, anon.)

'Just arrived?' asked the brightly uniformed officer.

'No, no,' said the young man in the worn dressing-gown. 'I've been here a few weeks now.'

'Feeling better?'

'A little.'

'So am I. When were you commissioned?'

'I'm a sergeant,' replied the young man indifferently. 'They couldn't find a bed in the NCOs' place so they sent me here.'

The officer looked away, apparently losing interest. About the same age, the pair were also similar in other ways – with their blue eyes, fresh complexions and sandy hair. The officer looked heavier, however, almost well fed.

'Seen any action?' asked the officer.

'Yes, some – I was at Mons in 1914.'

'Really? In the BEF, then?'

'I was part of the rearguard holding off the Germans.'

'Decorated for it?'

There was a pause.

'Yes', said the young man, 'the Victoria Cross.' Two of their six guns had been hit almost at once, he remembered. Later, through a hail of machine-gun bullets, bodies twirling and falling around them, they'd fed shells into their one remaining gun until the Germans had eventually withdrawn.

'James Crighton-Bannerman,' said the officer, his eyes brightening. 'My family home is in North Yorkshire. You sound as if you come from somewhere close by.'

'Yes, I've a small farm in the Dales. Anderson, Jake Anderson.'

The pair shook hands.

'My uncle is Henry Crighton-Bannerman, the MP. I've been in France myself. Staff officer, on temporary secondment, attached to the 9th Battalion, Royal Fusiliers. I'd be interested to see it some time.'

'See what?'

'Your Victoria Cross. It's good to meet a man who's bagged a few Huns.'

As Jake opened the door to his room, he took a last look at Crighton-Bannerman's bright scarlet cap band and collar tabs. 'The Red Badge of Funk,' he murmured to himself.

*   *   *   *

In Leeds, the first few months of the Great War had produced an atmosphere of restless excitement: everywhere men in khaki, flags fluttering, recruiting stations with posters demanding volunteers and bands playing to cheering troop trains. In the Dales, they'd come for Jake Anderson's workhorses first – never again would their feathery legs trample across his foldyard. Jake had followed his two shires to France shortly afterwards. Already familiar with guns and horses, he was soon promoted to sergeant.

Now he looked out of his bedroom window at the cloud shadow racing over the rolling, grassy chalk hills of Kent. The rounded downlands of Picardy were like this once, he thought. The big guns, the powerful artillery had reduced the French countryside to a desolate, shell-pitted waste. Two heavy horses were pulling a plough peacefully up a fold, the blades slicing a deep wound in the flinty brown earth. Same earth, same endless horror of what he'd seen, turning over and over in his mind. And what about his shires? Dead most likely, slaughtered in battle, their waste turned into glycerine and used to manufacture TNT.

There was a knock at the door and a young nurse entered the room.

At seventeen, Ilene Snaddon had travelled from Bradford in search of war work. She'd been a despatch rider for the Women's Emergency Corps, and worked as a conductor on the trams. Her pale skin and auburn hair were still tinged yellow from her last job filling shells with high explosives in a bomb-making factory. She'd then trained briefly as a nurse, and war-time demands for labour had quickly secured her a position in this hospital on the borders of Kent and Sussex.

'Would you like some more sleeping pills, Jake?' she asked brightly.

'No, I've a full bottle left. You could give me a haircut, though. The hospital barber gives me a convict crop.' Jake gave one of his rare smiles. 'And all the time he's cutting, he hums and whistles one of those jolly war songs that seem to be so popular this side of the Channel.'

As Ilene cut his hair, her cool fingers brushed his ears, his cheek, the warm nape of his neck. Once she held his chin in her hand, inspecting her handiwork closely.

Returning from the front line to rest is like this, thought Jake. First sleep and food to spread warmth throughout his tired body – then with those needs met his mind could turn to a woman.

In the fading evening light, the steady rumble of the guns was clearly heard across the Channel.

'It's hard to believe,' said Ilene.

'Believe what, Ilene?'

'That a war's so close,' she replied, simply.

Wild thoughts filled Jake's mind. He was lining up with other dirty, unshaven faces in a crumbling, water-logged trench – the sky a bayoneted slit of light. Then came the order: 'Fifteen minutes to go, boys'.

'I've heard the big offensive they're planning will end it all soon,' said Ilene, moving to the window to draw the curtains. A crescent moon hung low in the starry sky, cradling the faint outline of the old.

'A new moon,' said Jake, following her gaze.

'When I was a child, Father called it a new moon with the old moon in her arms. He said it was the sign of a deadly storm.' Ilene placed her scissors and combs into a small case. 'I must be going now. I'll put some of your haircut money into the collection tin for munitions.'

Halfway to the door she turned and began to sob – quietly at first, then louder and louder. The evening air had turned heavy, oppressive, the guns still rumbling like an imminent summer storm.

'What's the matter, Ilene?' asked Jake.

'They'll send me to the workhouse or a mental asylum.'

'Who will?' he said soothingly. 'Why?' Ilene was always cheerful. He'd never seen her distressed before. She fell to her knees at his side and he reached out to stroke the crown of her head, struck again by the unnatural colour of her hair.

'I'm going to have a baby,' she said.

'Oh!' said Jake.

'He found out.'

'Who? Found out what?'

'He threatened to tell the hospital unless I ...'

'Tell them what?' asked Jake, opening a drawer in search of a handkerchief. She paused and wiped her eyes.

'I've been in prison. It was while I was working in the munitions factory. There'd been a blackout the night before it all happened, and a friend, I forget who it was now, gave me a couple of matches to light a candle. I only used one. The next morning at work, I pulled some money from my pocket and a match dropped out. I tried to explain but no one would listen. They took me to court the next day. It was either twenty-eight days' imprisonment or a fine. I'd no money. My relatives were all in Yorkshire and I didn't want them to know. I couldn't stand the shame. So I was taken away to prison. When I got out I volunteered for nurse training – it's all I ever really wanted to do. The WVS gave me a good reference and I covered up – the prison sentence, that is – when I came here.'

'Who threatened to tell the authorities?' asked Jake.

'He told me to get rid of it, not to be a silly girl.'

'Who?'

'Mr Crighton-Bannerman,' said Ilene, starting to sob again.

*   *   *   *

Later that evening Ilene was called to Doctor Riley's room. Her eyes were still red from crying.

'Two escorts will arrive for Jake Anderson tomorrow evening,' said the doctor. 'In my opinion he has recovered sufficiently to return to France. Make sure that all his personal belongings are packed and that he is given any prescribed medication. Include some sleeping pills: I'll sign the prescription now. Is that quite clear?'

'The escorts?' Ilene was puzzled.

'None of your concern,' continued Riley, without looking up.

'He still shakes so, Doctor Riley, and he hardly sleeps.'

'That will do, Nurse Snaddon. I'll see Anderson now instead of tomorrow. Ask him to come through. That will be all.'

Riley was a fierce-looking man, even more bad tempered after an evening's drinking, and not to be questioned, so Ilene made no further comment, merely nodding compliantly before hurrying off to give Jake the news.

'You're going back to France,' she blurted out tearfully when she entered his room. 'Two escorts are coming for you tomorrow evening.'

Jake turned away, moved towards his bedside cupboard and slid open the top drawer. 'Crighton-Bannerman has been in,' he said. 'He wanted to look at this.'

He flung his Victoria Cross onto the bed and turned to face her.

'I once came across a German soldier in France – wounded by one of our snipers, I think. He was clearly dying, but he raised his arm feebly when he saw me. We were surrounded by filth: bomb craters filled deep with mud and rusted equipment; rotting horses; dead soldiers in heaps – faces hidden or grotesquely staring. The best I could do was to give him a drink of petrol-tainted water. He drank it, vomited and died. That's when I realised, more clearly than ever, that this thirst for other men's blood is all wrong. We've lost all reverence for living things. Pity that should be part of life's story. This war's the work of the devil. But there's something else too.'

'You don't have to talk about it now.'

'I may not get another chance if I'm leaving to-morrow. Some of our men were sent on a trench raid. It turned out to be a disaster. They returned in uniforms tattered and splattered with blood, stained yellow with lyddite, faces blackened and unshaven, swaying, shuffling from exhaustion, bent double, ready to lie down and die. One of the party, a soldier from somewhere in Yorkshire, just a boy really, was accused of cowardice. I visited him as often as I could during his detention. He told me he'd lied about his age so he could join up. At a service after the boy's execution, the padre talked about the 'purging power of death'. That was enough for me. I'd stopped saluting and standing to attention, which can count as a capital offence. A week or so later, they sent me here, even though I wasn't an officer. They said I might think differently after a while.'

'Those poor northern lads, so far away from home,' said Ilene. 'I always feel so sorry for them when I see them at the stations leaving for France.'

Jake paused to take a sip of water, his hand trembling.

'The General wouldn't change his decision. I was told he signed the execution order like a bank manager signing a loan agreement, while boys like young Andrew are standing for hours in the trenches, waist deep in mud with water seeping through their boots until their toes rot.'

'Here,' he said, picking up the Victoria Cross from the bed. 'Take this.'

* * * *

Ilene used a pestle to grind the tablets to a fine powder. She was sure he'd sleep soundly.

Later that night the escorts came.

'Here are his identity disc and some sleeping tablets,' said Ilene. 'You may need to give him some if he's restless during the crossing. He might become difficult to handle and start talking nonsense.'

The escorts smiled knowingly as they bent to lift the sleepy figure. 'Look,' said one, 'there's his Victoria Cross.'

Ilene leaned over the drowsy man and pulled up his greatcoat collar, shuddering as she rinsed two glasses on the bedside table with water from the jug. A few minutes later she roused another sleeping body. 'It's time to go,' she said. The moon was still new, crescent shaped, its faint halo enclosing the darkness of its predecessor.

'A new moon with the old moon in her arms,' he said.

She smiled: he'd remembered.

Early the following morning, 1 July 1916, on a cratered road approaching the Western Front, a London bus converted to military transport skidded, crashed and burst into flames: just two escorts survived. A Victoria Cross found in the greatcoat pocket of a dead man was later returned to London.

Meanwhile, just a few miles away on the Somme, British soldiers looked up at that same moon and prepared for a deadly storm.

AT TEA

The kettle descants in a cosy drone,
And the young wife looks in her husband's face,
And then in her guest's, and shows in her own
Her sense that she fills an envied place;
And the visiting lady is all abloom,
And says there was never so sweet a room.

(*At Tea*, Thomas Hardy)

'Stop here, by the lych-gate,' said Elizabeth. 'I'll walk to the rectory through the graveyard.'

She climbed down from the pony and trap. The autumn day was chilly, the pale watery sun no more than a halo behind a thin sheet of white cloud. Coarse stubble and brown ploughed earth swept upwards in gently contoured folds to the misty drizzle of the heathland above.

'When do you want me again, madam?' asked her driver. He was hoping for a warm drink, perhaps a meal in the rectory kitchen, before returning to the village in the next valley.

'The Devonshire Arms is open,' said Elizabeth. She allowed herself a small smile behind her wide-brimmed, veiled hat. 'Go in and warm yourself before you set off home.'

She handed him some coins, and his rheumy eyes brightened at the prospect of a glass of hot rum.

In the churchyard, Elizabeth stopped by a low, mildewed wall and stooped low to examine a new gravestone, that of a child who was born and died in a single year, 1899. She caught her wrist on a thorny briar amongst the nettles and a few drops of blood trickled onto the slab.

She stood and paused for a while, her young face seeming to age as she stared at the inscription – Acfield, her maiden name. Then she turned abruptly and continued to the rectory.

'Come in, Cousin, come in,' said Jane. 'Your visit is long overdue. We've hardly seen you since the wedding. You look so cold. First, a drink of tea to warm you through and then we shall take our meal.'

Finger by finger, Elizabeth peeled off her gloves, but she didn't remove her hat.

She recalled the previous occupant of the rectory: a pipe-smoking bachelor priest. The house had been untidy and unwelcoming, a place where the presence of stale smoke and unwashed dogs hung unpleasantly in the cold rooms. Now a fire glowed in the hearth and the whole house smelled of bread.

'You've been baking,' she said, turning to look admiringly at the floral pattern on the china teacups.

'A wedding present,' said Jane proudly. 'John likes them too.'

Elizabeth smiled, endeavouring to share her cousin's pleasure.

'And now you're married too,' said Jane, 'and to a wealthy man at that. A new start after all the ...'

'Yes,' replied Elizabeth. She lowered her eyes and concentrated on stirring her tea.

Silence ensued as the two women struggled to find something to say.

'John is in his study preparing his Advent sermon,' said Jane. 'He's giving it in the Minster – not here in the village church. I'll call him. You must look at our wedding photographs, and I've other gifts to show you.'

She departed and soon her husband came into the room.

Traces of churchyard mud clung to the hem of Elizabeth's dress. John moved towards her, but he wasn't certain what to do or say. Her dress made her seem shapely, voluptuous.

Upstairs, he could hear his straightforward, goodhearted wife moving around in her usual nervous way.

'The secret is ours,' said Elizabeth, placing a finger to her lips.

'I've seen the gravestone,' said John, sitting down opposite her. He wanted to be more to her than he was, but he knew it could never be. The clock ticked on monotonously, just as it did each evening when he and Jane sat together in this room.

'How fares your husband?' said John.

Carefully, Elizabeth removed her hat-pin and placed the wide-brimmed, veiled hat on the table. Her hair was plaited, pinned up – no longer falling loosely onto white shoulders – and one side of her face was bruised.

Just then Jane returned to the room with some photographs: 'Cousin, your face. Whatever can have happened?'

Slowly, Elizabeth raised her head.

'It was early this morning, as I was preparing for my visit. He accused me of seeing another. He lunged at me. It is not the first time.'

Tears filled her fine eyes.

Jane looked across at her husband. 'You must stay with us this evening,' she said.

'Thank you, but no. I've arranged for a room at the Devonshire Arms. I sail for the island in the morning. I've found employment there.' She smiled faintly and sipped her tea. 'That's better. I'm glad I've told you.'

*   *   *   *

Early the following morning John left his wife asleep in their bed and strode the flinty byways to the Devonshire Arms, cleric's cloak flapping in the wind. Behind him, his advent sermon lay discarded on the study floor – thick, erratic lines scored diagonally across each page.

JUST AROUND THE CORNER

Ann looked down on her four children as they waited together on the crowded platform. Evacuation had been discussed for so long, but now it was a reality. The youngsters would soon be waving goodbye to her and their familiar life in their small Yorkshire town.

She knew Douglas was apprehensive, but he was trying to be brave in front of his younger brother Billy and two small sisters, Lucy and Lydia.

'Is Father still upset?' asked Douglas.

Ann swallowed hard. A short letter had informed them that Katherine's ship had been torpedoed and sunk just off the Donegal coast. Leslie had given his sister the fare, thinking she and her baby would be safe from danger with relatives in Canada. The Germans claimed to have mistaken the liner for an armed merchant-cruiser. Then a broken pulley had sent the lifeboat nose-diving into the sea. Katherine had managed to scramble back aboard, but her baby was gone.

'Remember to keep your gas masks dry and out of the rain,' said Ann. The masks frightened Lucy and Lydia. The girls hated putting them on, and all the children loathed the smell of the clinging, claustrophobic rubber. 'There are sandwiches for the journey,' their mother continued. She had prepared them with the usual Bovril spread thinly over the bread.

The train pulled in and the station began to fill with steam. Ann's eyes roved over her four children as she checked that their brown identification labels were securely tied.

'Who's Lord Haw Haw, Mother?' asked ten-year-old Billy.

'What a time to ask. Why do you want to know?'

'John Drayton said he'd listened to Lord Haw Haw on the wireless. He said Lord Haw Haw was a traitor.'

'Don't you worry about that now,' said Ann. She was remembering the night an incendiary bomb had crashed through the ceiling of the children's room and lodged between two beds. Leslie had grabbed it and thrown it out of the window. Painful red scars had covered his hands for a couple of months, and he had needed regular hospital treatment until they improved.

'You're going to the countryside,' Ann continued. 'It's safer there. To a village in the Dales – not too far away.' She thought of them all huddled around the wireless as the slow, sombre tones of Neville Chamberlain announced that the war had begun. Sirens had blared the following night. It had been a false alarm, but now her palms grew moist and her stomach fluttered whenever she heard that sound. Thankfully, the children would be well out of the way next time.

She smoothed her daughters' hair and straightened their coat collars. According to the local papers, many of the evacuees were infected with head lice.

Sunlight filtered through the dirty glass in the arched station roof, turning the steam yellow. A few carriage doors had begun to slam. They looked up at the large clock with its ornate ironwork. 'We've a few minutes yet,' said Douglas. 'Don't worry, Mother. I'll take care of us all.'

'I know you will,' said Ann. The skin around her eyes was tight and drawn. 'You can sit next to the Hargreaves' children on the train. And look, over there – isn't that John Drayton? You'll be able to chat to him too.'

'They don't talk to us anymore,' said Billy.

'Why not?' asked Ann.

'They wouldn't say,' said Billy. He looked away, suddenly subdued. 'Father was very brave, wasn't he?'

'Is Father away because of the war?' asked Lydia.

'Of course he is,' said Billy. 'All my friends' fathers are fighting in the war.'

'Uncle Jack wore a uniform,' said Douglas, 'but he was in the Merchant Navy.'

'Yes,' said his mother quietly. Shortly after the incendiary had crashed into their home, Leslie's brother Jack had been returning from his first deep-sea voyage – homeward bound across the North Atlantic with a cargo of Canadian grain – when his ship was attacked and sunk by U-boats. Jack had attended the local grammar school and would soon have received command of his own vessel. Leslie had done his best, but his mother was inconsolable at the loss of her youngest son.

'We used to like it when Father played the piano,' said Lucy.

'And when he teased us,' said Lydia.

Douglas glanced down the train as doors slammed and windows opened for final embraces. 'We've got to get in now,' he said.

Once the guard had blown his whistle and waved his flag, departures were hurried and words few. Then the train pulled slowly away, leaving Ann engulfed in a cloud of billowing grey smoke.

A heavy downpour just minutes earlier had left the pavements brilliant with the reflections of dazzling sunlight. At the Tower, Shirley Temple was starring in *Just Around the Corner*; meanwhile outside the Carlton, a poster advertised *Trouble Brewing*. George Formby strummed his ukulele and looked down benignly. Ann smiled at his foolish, toothy grin, and then at the thought of the comical faces of Hitler and Mussolini.

In the west, clouds were invading the skies and veiling the sun, now dropping behind factories and tall chimney stacks. The nightly blackout would soon plunge the town into a starry darkness.

Leslie had been a man of some standing in the community – as scoutmaster, sportsman and musician. When war broke out, he had just returned from the annual scout camp at Bridlington. He opened the batting for the cricket team and, as bandmaster, he'd taken part in every event of the town's centenary celebrations. Ann smiled again: Leslie had been exhausted by the end of that hot July day.

Leslie had hated the war, with its ever-tightening grip of regulation and restriction. Then came the loss of his niece and his brother. And after the injuries he suffered in the incendiary attack, he lost interest in playing the piano.

Ann recalled their last day together in the countryside. It had been late spring. In the dappled light of a copse, fragrant wild garlic had gleamed like patches of winter snow. Hundreds of butterflies had flitted or basked among the grass and wildflowers of a sunny meadow. 'Look there,' Leslie had said playfully to his children, pointing out a Duke of Burgundy among the cowslips and bluebells. 'Quickly, before you miss it.' He was all too aware that his town, like so many others, was perched on the edge of an abyss as the country drifted towards war.

*   *   *   *

Ann turned her key in the door and entered a house made dark by the blacked-out windows. The words of the magistrate at the petty sessions came back to her again. His withering contempt for her pacifist husband made her shudder. Then her spirits lifted slightly. Leslie had been sent to work on a farm and tomorrow she would visit him there. At least, she reflected grimly, it was an improvement on the mental hospital and the prison which had gone before it.

THE LAST TANGO

'Other competitors say I remind them of Ginger Rogers when they see me on the dance floor,' she said coyly, lowering her thickly layered eyelids. Her blue-green mascara had already started to run, adding streaks of oily colour to her flushed face and perspiring, mottled neck.

I was chatting to her in the cooler air of the foyer. 'Really,' I replied politely, an unconvincing ring to my voice. I'd seen her carrot-coloured hair before, bobbing up and down at dance competitions in the city, but it had never occurred to me to compare this lady with the elegant Ginger.

'My name is Le Vogier,' she said. Her voice was irritating and affected. 'Mademoiselle Le Vogier because I'm not married. It's French, you know.'

She extended her podgy hand for me to shake. Her fingernails were long and polished, deep red. But her hand felt clammy and I quickly released it.

She was beginning to attract attention, her voice becoming shrill.

'It's not my real name,' she squealed. 'I only use it when I dance in competitions with Fred. When other entrants say how unusual it is, I tell them I'm from Paris. Fred and I went there last year and – can you believe it? – we danced in the street. He looked so handsome in his black pin-striped suit and white spats. After all the years we've been together I thought he might just propose.'

I glanced at my watch, praying my partner would return soon.

'Fred says he can't even think about marriage yet,' she continued. 'He's far too busy with his business. Sometimes I don't see him for months on end. It was his business that took us to Paris. My father wanted to call me Evelyn after a woman he'd known, but I ended up plain Josephine, Josephine Sidebottom. Friends at home call me Jo, but I don't like that at all. It sounds too masculine, and I'm not a bit masculine, am I?'

Over on the far side of the foyer, Jim Scott was demonstrating a dance step to a crowd of young admirers so there was no point in trying to attract his attention.

'I think this Evelyn was part of a *ménage à trois* with my father and mother. There you go, French again. It keeps coming out – must be in the genes somewhere.'

'Paris,' I ventured, feeling I had to say something. 'You must have found it quite an experience returning to your land of origin.' Then I remembered the swarthy face of the man I'd seen dancing with this lady earlier in the evening. 'Does your partner come from abroad as well?'

We paused briefly to watch the willowy movements of young couples dancing the rumba.

'All our cups and trophies are for Latin-American,' boasted Mademoiselle Le Vogier. 'It's far more sensuous when Fred and I dance it, though.'

Earlier that evening, Mademoiselle Le Vogier, née Sidebottom, legs like mature tree trunks, had teetered confidently onto the dance floor in her high-heeled shoes. She somehow seemed lighter as the music took hold and she began to glide around the room with her partner.

'Fred made a big display case for all our trophies,' she continued. 'It's in my front room. He asked me to put some of his prizes from singing competitions in there too. Did I tell you Fred has a fine baritone voice? No, no – I didn't. Anyway, a few months ago, late one night, he brought round a gold carriage clock. It had a pendulum that spins round and round – just like I do in a waltz. I put it in the display case with the rest of his clocks. Sometimes he brought cases of wine – far more than I could possibly drink. I had to store them all upstairs.'

'How kind,' I replied. This was all very embarrassing: much longer and the other dancers would start thinking Mademoiselle Le Vogier was my partner.

'I'm terribly particular about my appearance and I'm careful who I talk to,' she said, hastily reapplying her vivid lipstick and smoothing her carrotty hair. A black bow drew it together at the back of her head – a style more suitable, I thought, for those lissom young ladies I'd seen swaying around the floor only a few moments earlier.

'I can see you've kept yourself in trim,' I said, doing my best to flatter her. Her fleshy midriff was visibly wobbling under her black chiffon two-piece dress.

'It was my idea to donate some of Fred's prizes to local dance competitions,' she said. 'I didn't think he'd mind. There were so many of them. I'd four or five clocks, several cases of wine and some boxes I hadn't even opened. I thought we could have the engraving scratched off the rose bowl and present it as the Frederick and Mona Le Vogier Tango Cup. One of the carriage clocks could go to the best couple in the rumba. And I included a box of wine for the raffle.'

'Again very generous,' I replied.

'There were dance teams from the Royal Infirmary, the City Engineers, the Oil Refinery, Rollet and Farson – the solicitors, Customs and Excise and the City CID, who do a very good military two-step. I told Fred what I'd done during a quickstep. For some reason he became confused. He completely lost his rhythm, which isn't like Fred, and then he excused himself.'

'Who won?' I asked.

'Well, the CID team won the rose bowl; Customs and Excise, the wine; and the solicitors, the carriage clock. They thanked me for my generosity, but I didn't want to take all the credit. Oh no, I said, the man you must really thank is my partner Fred Hornby, who's in business in the city.'

'Look!' I said. 'Over there, someone's waving to you. It must be Fred.'

'Oh no, that's not Fred,' she said. 'He never did turn up for the last tango and I haven't seen him since. It upset me for ages. I suppose he could have gone away on business again.' But any sadness in her voice was only fleeting. 'I'm with Ernest now,' she continued gaily. 'With my looks and dancing ability new partners have never been a problem.' And on that note Mademoiselle Le Vogier took her leave and teetered back onto the dance floor.

THE PRINTER'S DEVIL

Robert Laban Laister was a well-known figure in the town. Manager of the Theatre Royal since 1897, he also designed all the sets and posters, putting to good use an artistic talent inherited from his mother, herself a gifted pianist and watercolour painter.

After his usual lunchtime drink in the Rose, Robert was returning in late afternoon to his small terraced house, swinging his gold-knobbed cane and reciting to himself a few lines he'd overheard at rehearsal. He could be amusing in this kind of mood. He was popular with visiting theatre companies but often hasty and hot-tempered with his family.

Robert walked unsteadily into the front room, sat down with a bump and greeted his wife: 'You've had your dinner already, I see.'

'You're late,' snapped Ellen Laister. 'I waited as long as I could. The doctor told me I need to eat regularly. I've kept it warm for you.'

'It looks a bit dried up to me.' He gestured theatrically for her to take the plate away. 'I'll have some bread and cheese and a bottle of Connor's Ale instead.'

'There is no ale, Robert. I can go and fetch some from Hattersley's if you want.'

'No, no need to trouble yourself. The bread and cheese'll do.'

Later on he slept. Ellen sighed deeply and stroked his thinning head of hair. She reached over and poked the fire, the only point of brightness in the sparsely furnished room. Robert would wake shortly and feel the chill. The slight movement roused him a little and brought her a mumbled apology. In a few hours, he'd be back at the theatre – a touring company were performing Romeo and Juliet. But Ellen would let him rest a while yet.

*   *   *   *

Esther Moore's official position at the Theatre Royal was that of cleaner, but with her alert eye for detail she had soon acquired extra duties. No one seemed to mind: least of all the owner, a retired industrialist with little interest in the Royal. Whenever there was a crisis, everyone turned to this practical young woman who lived in a small flat above the main entrance.

'Leave what you're doing,' Robert told her late one afternoon. He took his pocket watch from his waistcoat and gave it a glance. 'We've got some posters to collect from the printer's and they shut at six. I promised the secretary of the Scientific and Literary Institute that I'd have them put up around town. They're for a lecture on Friday evening by Sir Charles Vernon, the Liberal MP. He's talking about eugenics. The room at the Institute isn't big enough, so I offered them use of the theatre. People will be coming from all over Yorkshire, and beyond. There'll be at least one bishop, and some of those serious-minded clergymen who take such a dim view of the rest of humanity.'

'Eugenics,' said Esther. 'What's that?'

'It's almost a new religion for some intellectuals and politicians. Only the elite should be allowed to breed, they reckon. They wouldn't let anyone else have children.'

'How would that work?' said Esther. 'Where would we find riveters like my grandfather? Who would work in the mines, or the quarries, or in shipbuilding?' She set aside the dress she was repairing and reached for her coat. 'Or finish off the needlework on this costume for that matter?'

'Come to the meeting and ask.'

'Will any other women be there?'

'Not many. I've only ever seen the odd one or two, and then not at every meeting.'

Robert reached for a couple of bags for the posters.

'You've cancelled amateurs' music hall night, then?' asked Esther. The regular, rowdy, smoke-filled Friday evenings were open to all. 'Do you want me to get the hooked pole and stand in the wings so I can drag Sir Charles off stage if necessary? Some of the shipyard workers got a bit rowdy last Friday and threw rivets at the turns.'

*   *   *   *

The weather was threatening rain as they crossed the common pastures on the way back from the printer's. A handful of molten gashes split the dark clouds fast gathering in the west. The sudden downpour soaked them through and sent them running for the theatre.

'I'll make you a drink,' said Esther, shivering as they climbed the stairs to her flat. 'You'll dry off in no time in my sitting-room.'

'You should have a hot bath first,' said Robert.

'Here, hang your things to dry on this clothes-horse.' Esther turned to fill two large pans standing on metal trivets. 'These won't take long to heat.'

Her movements were quick. The room filled with shadow from the fire and light from the gas mantle, while outside the rain hammered against the window.

'They're like thousands and thousands of lives,' said Robert.

'What are?' asked Esther

'Those beads of rainwater racing down the window: they surface brightly and then eventually disappear.'

'You can be ever so serious, Robert.'

When the water was hot, Esther gave Robert a small cloth to protect his hands while he lifted the pans. 'The bath's through there,' she said, pointing towards an open door.

As he listened to the sounds of Esther bathing, Robert's thoughts turned to his wife. Ellen would be at home, cold and alone. She never acted on impulse. Arranging a vase of flowers might bring pleasure to her eyes, but little else.

Robert got up to feel his clothes. 'These are dry enough now,' he called out.

'Are you sure you wouldn't like a bath?' said Esther. 'You could use my water. Heat another pan up.'

He imagined her eyes would be shining like those beads of rainwater on the darkened glass. 'No thanks,' said Robert. 'I must get home.'

Returning to his chair, he caught a glimpse of Esther – the long curve of her naked back, the white petticoat hanging loosely from her slender waist, and the reflection of her face in a small mirror. The nearby dressing-table held the objects she handled every day: a clumsy water jug and wash-basin, hair-brushes, combs and inexpensive scents.

'I'd like to paint you,' said Robert suddenly. He had to capture her like this.

'Now?' she asked, powdering her face. 'How do would you want me to pose?'

'With your back to me,' he said. 'I'd like to see your face reflected in the mirror.'

She unpinned her hair, carelessly put up with whatever she had to hand.

'No, no pin it back up again,' said Robert. 'With that knot of hair tied at the back.'

He dashed downstairs to the theatre below to gather paints, easel and canvas. 'Your skin's slightly tawny,' he remarked on his return. 'Why is that?'

'A tawny owl.' She winked at him and her laughter filled the room. 'My grandmother once told me that her mother fell in love with a Spanish seaman. There used to be a shipping line round here that sailed to northern Spain.'

She paused. 'I've something to ask you, Robert. Did I ever mention that I've joined the Women's Suffrage Society?'

'You're not a suffragette, are you? I read the other day that one woman has slashed a painting in an art gallery and another threw an axe at a politician.'

'No, no, we're not suffragettes, we're suffragists. We have some links with Emmeline Pankhurst and her group, but we're part of the National Union of Women's Suffrage Societies. We're a much larger organisation and we're trying to change opinions in a non-violent way. We want women to live more interesting lives. We want them to have the chance to do the same work as men. My branch is organising a regional meeting. Would you let us use the theatre?'

Robert looked thoughtful.

'You don't want us here, do you? You don't mind the men in the Scientific and Literary Institute holding meetings, but not a women's group.'

He turned away.

'I'll let you paint me, if you'll let us hire the theatre.'

'If I do, can you guarantee there'll be no heckling or disruption when Sir Charles Vernon speaks on Friday?'

'I can try, but our members are very strong minded. And Sir Charles will be talking about women having babies, so we should have some say in the matter.'

Later, on his way home, Robert recalled the evening with pleasure – and no little torment.

*   *   *   *

Ellen Laister filled the pot with water from the kettle.

'Here, let me do that,' said her son Lewis. The teapot was large and heavy, and her arms stick thin. Her hair, usually so dark and shiny, had recently grown quite dull.

'I've made you some beef sandwiches,' said Ellen. 'The meat was for your father, but he hasn't come home for his dinner. Have you seen him? It's very late.'

'No, I haven't,' replied Lewis, with some embarrassment. He knew his father met Esther in a busy public house: he'd seen them sometimes through the misted window, sentimental and patriotic music pouring out into the street. 'I've got news for you, Mother,' he continued. 'I've decided to leave the printing shop.'

'I thought Old John Lazenby had offered you an apprenticeship.'

'He has, but I don't want to take it.'

'I'm too tired to discuss it this evening,' said Ellen. 'Would you read to me before your father comes home? That piece of writing, the one you illustrated with your drawings. I can sit up in bed.'

Slowly they climbed the stairs, resting on the landing so she could regain her breath. He found an extra pillow to support her head and read to her for a while, but her eyes soon closed and she turned on her side.

They opened again briefly when Lewis kissed her forehead.

'You are clever, Lewis. You've always been kind, son.' He drew the blankets further over her. 'Lock the door, would you? I don't know what time your father will be home.'

In the backyard Lewis gazed up at the night sky and the refracted pink glow from the blast furnaces thirty miles distant. Closer to home, the Minster with its two mighty west towers looked in outline like a Viking longship. Soon he heard the familiar sound of his father's voice: loud and foolish after an evening's drinking.

'A printer's devil, a humble cleaner – is that the extent of your ambitions?' Robert berated his son. 'When I spoke to Old Lazenby the other day, he said he'd offered you an apprenticeship. My mother's family were all schoolteachers – two generations. Great-grandfather was the first person in the village who could read and write. Everyone would come to him for help.'

'I don't want to be a teacher or an apprentice, or to work on Old Lazenby's antiquated presses,' Lewis replied. Printing was John Lazenby's life. If Lewis took up the apprenticeship, Lazenby wouldn't hesitate to heap more work upon him. The printer's whining voice always contrived to make Lewis feel guilty, but he didn't want to hurt the old man's feelings. Lazenby had congratulated Lewis once or twice when the boy had noticed errors before work went to print.

Robert went into the house but Lewis decided to stay outside a while. For his mother's sake, he didn't want to risk any further confrontation with his father. A few leaves gusted around. Beyond the town, autumn was tightening its gentle hold – in the country lanes, in the warp lands, and on the river that brought in the laden ships from across the North Sea. Ploughed land gleamed in the pale light – pools of water landlocked between the furrows.

Life seemed bleak to Lewis: long, monotonous hours of work in the printing room, his mother in poor health, and his father living such a dissipated existence.

*   *   *   *

A few day after the funeral, Esther took a theatre bill to the printer's. Lewis was alone in the shop, still shocked by his father's sudden demise. Robert had died in the Theatre Royal and Esther had seen it happen.

'How are you?' she asked, placing a consoling hand on the boy's arm.

'Alright, I suppose. Mother hasn't been too well though.'

'It all happened so quickly.' Esther handed Lewis the poster. 'Sorry if this upsets you. It's one of your father's.'

'Don't worry. We're very busy though. How many copies do you need? And when do you want them?'

'Early next week will do.'

'We'd get them done much quicker if Old Lazenby would replace these museum pieces. I'll stop the current job and run them off for you.'

He reached towards one of the old presses. Esther turned to leave but was halted by a sudden cry.

'Help!' screamed Lewis. 'Grab the dead man's handle!'

*   *   *   *

They next met under the arch of the town's last remaining medieval gateway.

'Please let me help you, Lewis,' said Esther.

'What can you do?' he shouted, waving his mangled left hand. 'Even Old Lazenby has lost interest in me since the accident. I've overheard him telling his friends how I work too slowly to be an apprentice. He only keeps me on out of sympathy.'

'There's a lot more to do in the theatre now, and the manager needs someone else to work front of house and look after the publicity. You're artistic like your father. You could design all the posters.'

Lewis's time as a printer's devil would soon be at an end.

*   *   *   *

'Run upstairs would you, Lewis?' asked Reginald Segrott, the new manager of the Theatre Royal, and an impatient, demanding figure. 'Ask Esther to come down and see me.'

Esther was alone when he approached the open door of her flat. She crouched unawares on the floor, surrounded by costumes, absorbed in her work and strikingly beautiful, even in her everyday clothes.

'I'm never short of a job,' she said when Lewis knocked.

'Mr Segrott would like to see you,' he said. His eyes strayed over her head to a painting of a young woman completing her toilet, the very image of Esther as she bowed her head over her sewing.

Esther smiled, following the direction of his gaze.

Lewis turned to leave. 'Would you like us to hang that painting in the foyer?' he said. The words had come tumbling out. Just the idea of it brought a smile to his face.

'Yes. Yes, I would.'

*   *   *   *

The painting drew admiring glances from many a theatre-goer. Whenever she was questioned about it, Esther would reply simply that it was the work of a local artist. Then her face would break into the smile that had so entranced Robert Laister, and Lewis would think of his father rather more fondly than before.

THE INVITATION

A bright pool of light from the large, arched window drew the eyes of the two elderly men as they moved beyond the darkness of the main entrance. The heavy door closed with a thud, startling them both. A metal latch clanked, then finally slotted into place.

In the city streets outside, it was a cold November day of dark clouds, brief bursts of sunshine, and sudden squally showers driven in on a biting north-easterly.

'Glad to be out of that wind,' said Stan.

'Switch on the lights, for goodness sake,' said his companion Archie, waving his walking stick towards the switches by the door. Archie had been a serviceman for many years and was used to giving orders. The flight of stone steps outside had left him slightly out of breath, and wispy swirls of vapour rose from his mouth in the cold interior.

'No lights,' said Stan, flicking the switches repeatedly.

'Stop that,' said Archie.

'No heating either,' said Stan, shivering.

The cold air seemed to be coming straight up from the stone floor.

Stan took a cigarette butt from the side of his mouth. It didn't seem right to smoke in here. Saliva glistened on his droopy, tobacco-stained moustache. Reaching out in the gloom, his hand met the smooth, cold surface of a marble effigy and the feel of it made him shudder.

'Roof's high,' said Archie, his tone hushed as he looked up towards the delicate vaulting. A carved face with the mocking, wide, upturned mouth of a clown looked down upon him.

Both men reverently removed their hats and smoothed their hands through their thinning grey hair.

'Do we have to keep our voices down?' said Stan.

'Yes,' replied Archie. 'You feel you've got to be quiet in a place like this.' Their footsteps echoed in the silence until they reached a thickly carpeted area. Somewhere above them a clock ticked unseen in its measured, timeless way.

'Well, the glasses are out on the tables, at least' said Stan, pointing his rolled-up newspaper towards a highly polished mahogany table.

A sudden knocking startled the two men.

'Only the central heating system,' said Archie. 'It must be on a timer today. Mavis said they're serving the free meal for pensioners at twelve. We're still a bit early.'

A sudden squall pattered against the glass and the arched window lost its radiance. A crack of thunder sounded and they waited expectantly for the first flash of lightning. Then light and darkness interchanged until the thunder eventually rumbled away and the window was bathed once again in a pool of white.

'Perhaps we should go,' said Stan. He found the patch of brightness on the otherwise dark wall most unsettling. 'That light over there, don't you think it's odd?'

'No,' said Archie. 'It's just a reflection – perhaps from the mirrors behind those bottles.'

'Look,' said Stan. 'There's a door in the far corner. Could be someone working there, I suppose.'

They went to investigate. 'Dark in here, too,' said Archie, pulling back a thick black velvet curtain and sneezing loudly from the dust. A pile of old registers lay open on another mahogany table and a painting hung on the wall. It showed the serene figure of a man in flowing garb standing beside a closed door; a lantern shone bright in his hand.

'*Light of the World,*' said Archie.

'You what?' asked Stan, checking some candles he'd found in a box. 'I suppose we might get a bit of light from these until someone comes.' He wanted to hear voices and laughter: this darkness made him very uncomfortable.

'Do you see those empty bottles?' said Archie, annoyed that it was Stan who had come up with the suggestion. 'We'll put the candles in those.'

'That's better,' he continued, as they watched streaks of yellow candlelight dance up the stone walls. 'I'm sure someone will be here soon. Mavis doesn't usually get things wrong.' Maybe it was his imagination, but he was sure that patch of light on the wall was growing larger.

The clock chimed quarter past the hour. It creaked and strained as the ancient mechanism rewound itself.

Then the knocking started again. The patch of light on the wall grew bigger still and the mouths of those carved stone faces became even more ghastly. Glass splintered, a sudden gust of wind blew out most of the candles – and Archie and Stan fled in terror. Then, as the front door slammed shut behind them, the last remaining candle fell onto Stan's paper and a pile of dry, dusty books.

*　　*　　*　　*

'The Fire Brigade reckon it's arson,' said Mavis in the kitchen the following day. She pointed to a photograph in the late edition of the local paper. A fireman was holding two hats and a walking stick. 'It's a real shame. Today was meant to be the official opening.'

'Today?' replied Archie, trying not to show his unease. He didn't want his wife guessing that they'd turned up on the wrong date. 'I always thought it shouldn't be allowed.'

'What shouldn't be allowed?'

'Turning a church into a cafe,' replied Archie, shivering at the memory of the wind, the darkness and the sound of shattering glass as he and Stan had made their hurried exit from St Barnabas'.

THE HEALTH OF THE BRIDE

The long wooden bench on one side of the table and the chairs for close family on the other were beginning to feel bone hard to the guests when William Blanchard finally rose to his feet.

His sister Harriett raised a bony finger to her lips for quiet.

William turned to the bride and pointed to the porcelain dinner service laid out on the gleaming white tablecloth before him. 'When I'm dead and gone, they'll all be for you, Jessie my child.'

'Tis a wedding feast, not a funeral wake,' snapped Harriett.

A crimson tide spread over William's thick neck and forehead. He leaned heavily on the table and fumbled in his waistcoat pocket for the speech he'd rehearsed earlier. It had been a mistake to blurt out the first thing that came into his head.

'And that's not all, Jessie,' said William. Again he was departing from his prepared script, confusing the order and moving straight to the climax. 'There's something else for you in the inn yard.'

Jessie left the room, and a gentle hum of conversation resumed around the table.

'What a beautiful mare, Uncle William,' she said on her return.

'I know it's your heart's desire.'

Aunt Harriett frowned, and the other guests fell silent.

'She has another heart's desire now,' said cousin John Stanley. 'We mustn't forget her new husband. Wed only an hour ago.' Laughter rippled through the room. 'I propose a toast to the bride and groom. May they know nothing but health and prosperity. Please raise your glasses to Jessie and Henry.'

'Thank you, John,' said William. He was feeling giddy, the fluttering in his chest more frequent. His thick woollen suit – worn at Harriett's insistence – was hot and uncomfortable. His tie felt tight, like the cord closing off a sack of flour in one of his mills.

'Good health to you, Jessie,' said William, beaming at his niece's evident happiness. 'And you too, Henry. Mind you take good care of her.'

The meal over, William made his way to the opposite end of the table, where Walter Langley sat with his arm around his pig-tailed grand-daughter.

The child slipped quickly away.

'Still keeping a few hives?' Walter asked.

'A few here and there.' replied William. 'Time drags so since my Esther died.'

'I understand,' said Walter. He lowered his voice and looked around. 'Have you heard the County Bank is in difficulties?'

'Difficulties,' asked William. 'What sort of difficulties?' He had money in the County – only the other day he'd called in to make a withdrawal for the wedding – and he was also a shareholder. When the manager had approached him for a donation, he'd even given money to convert part of the workhouse into a hospital.

'The County's been buying up some of the smaller banks,' continued Walter, with his twisted smile. 'There have been some bankruptcies around here. Old Peter Dunning and others haven't repaid their loans, and that's a fact. I reckon the bank has overstretched itself.'

'That can't be right,' said William.

'I hear you've made another big donation to the hospital.'

'It's my money,' snapped William. 'I can do with it as I please.'

Walter nodded towards Jessie, now dancing to a lively violin tune. 'Your niece is like a queen bee on her wedding flight.'

'That she is,' said William.

'When does Harriett go home?'

'In a week's time – when Jessie returns from honeymoon.'

Walter ran his hand over his shiny bald head, a knowing gleam in his sharp, bird-like eyes. 'Harriett says Jessie will be away for two weeks. That's how she spent the money you gave her. Harriett thinks a week away should be long enough for anyone.'

Unable to hide his surprise, William moved off.

*   *   *   *

William left the celebrations early, feeling tired and breathless. He pushed hard at the door, forgetting the boxes of honey stacked behind it. More boxes lined the corridor outside, leaving only a narrow passageway. Harriett had scolded him on her arrival. Papers, letters and old newspapers littered the bureau and table, and dusty ledgers and boxes of invoices were piled high in the corners, some in his father's copperplate hand: a hard man, James Blanchard – always reluctant to offer praise.

The bureau contained letters from his wife. William sighed. Where was she now? Beyond joy? Beyond pain? He lay thinking about her every night. Harriett had been the only one to visit them. Husband and wife had fed off one another like two bees sharing a cell in a honeycomb.

William sat in his chair, running his hands through his grey hair. Why hadn't Jessie rushed over and kissed him when she'd seen the horse? William was by no means an emotional man, but his eyes grew suddenly wet with tears. It had been a long day. Thank goodness Harriett would be back shortly. He took a few papers from the cluttered table and added them to the pile on the chair next to him.

He would contact the County Bank and withdraw some of the money on deposit there. He wouldn't take it all out – just make sure Jessie had cash in case the bank went into liquidation. He'd write and tell her where he'd hidden it. Might the other banks also be in trouble? Perhaps he'd better contact them as well. William started to write but soon his eyes grew heavy.

Harriett found him sleeping and covered him with a blanket. He grunted as she placed a cushion under his head.

'My brother,' she sighed, stroking his hair and despairing at the state of the house and room. She could never persuade him to change.

*   *   *   *

'Nineteen, twenty, that's another hundred,' William said to himself, tying a length of string around a bundle of carefully folded notes. He had soon set to work withdrawing money from his accounts. Walter Langley was a shrewd man, usually right when it came to financial matters. Harriett would receive a lifetime annuity, but everything else would go to Jessie. William, however, was angry with her. His niece had visited only once since her honeymoon

29

and still had not sent a letter of thanks for his gifts. He made several attempts to write to her, only to tear up each sheet in a rage.

* * * *

One afternoon in early May, William emerged from the County Bank into a biting easterly wind. It was raining hard and drifts of wet pink blossom covered the pathways. Nearby, three children and a young woman were sheltering under a torn umbrella.

'I don't like to ask, sir.' The young woman spoke with a soft Scottish accent. Her features were fine and feminine, but a few lines of tiredness clustered around her pale blue eyes.

William walked a few paces beyond the huddled group, then turned. 'Ask what?' he said.

'My children are hungry.'

Cold too, by the look of their thin clothes, thought William.

'My husband worked as a joiner in the naval shipyard at Seaton.' The young woman's eyes filled with tears. 'He lost his job and now he's searching for work. We haven't heard from him in weeks. We're in lodgings, in rooms above an undertaker's. My children are taunted constantly.'

'We don't sleep in coffins, sir,' said the boy.

William patted his tousled fair head. 'Come,' he said, sheltering the family under his large umbrella. 'I know an inn.'

* * * *

William's friendship with Mary and her children deepened. She visited him at home and showed an interest in his bees, watching him raise the queens by grafting larvae into artificial cell cups. William explained the insect's anatomy to the children, then watched them draw pictures of bees with bulging eyes and pendulous antennae.

Several weeks later he visited his solicitor.

'Her name is Mary Eves,' he said to the senior partner, Edward Wraithby-Brown. 'She has three children.'

Wraithby-Brown peered over his half-moon glasses. William had been seen around town with this young woman and her children. They were fast becoming a talking point.

'I'd like you to give Mary this letter in the event of my death,' continued William. 'I'd also like to make a gift to her now – a small property in town with an acre of rough land. It's been empty for some time. Otherwise my will remains the same.'

'I'll make the amendments and let you know when you can come in to sign,' said Wraithby-Brown.

* * * *

William, Mary and the children had walked out onto the chalk headland together. The gusty wind from the sea had made him gasp. Now he stood talking to Helen, the youngest child.

'Mother, Mother, come quickly,' she cried. 'Mr Blanchard has fallen. He is quite still.'

William's eyes were misty and vacant, his head cushioned by the springy grass and the fragrant wild thyme. The only sound came from the waves breaking steadily over sand and shingle.

A few days later Jessie and Henry visited Edward Wraithby-Brown's office, where the solicitor read out her uncle's will.

'You are still practically the sole beneficiary,' he said. 'Properties, some bank deposits and investments – all yours. You should be rich, young lady. There is, however, something else I should mention.'

Wraithby-Brown paused, cleared his throat and slowly refilled his glass with water.

'Your uncle kept beehives on some rough land behind a small terraced house. He recently gifted it to a young lady, Mary Eves. It doesn't amount to much.'

Jessie's face clouded with displeasure.

'These bank deposits are rather small,' said Henry.

*   *   *   *

Later that week Mary Eves received William's letter. It contained the key to the cellar, locked when the family had moved into the house. The news that she would find boxes down there made her tremble.

That same evening Mary heard a knock at the door. It was Walter Langley.

'Old John Framlington is in need of some company,' he said. 'Young female company preferred.'

DAVID

The lorry driver saw the sign and pulled off the road into the pitch-black lay-by. With a glance at his filthy dashboard clock, he rested his elbows on the huge steering wheel and followed his headlights into the darkness.

'This is as far as I can take you. Walk straight along the main street to the top of the village and you'll come to the main road. You might get a lift there. It's a bit late though, and it is Christmas Eve.'

David yawned and stretched.

'Didn't you say you come from round here?' continued the driver. 'Then you'll know the way already. Relatives in Hemley, wasn't it?'

'Yes, but that was a few years ago.' David rubbed his dirty hand over his shaven head. He'd just got comfortable, and it was with some difficulty that he eased himself out of the sunken, fake-leather seat and opened the door to the silent countryside beyond.

'Don't forget this,' said the driver, tossing down a red beret with a brass army badge. 'It's cold out there.' He picked up a shiny, beribboned silver cross lying on the passenger seat. 'This too, it must have slipped from your pocket.' In the light from the cabin, the driver finally noticed the disfigurement that marked one side of his passenger's face. 'Crikey,' he asked. 'How did that happen?'

'It's a long story, perhaps another time,' said David, turning away quickly.

'My great-grandfather was maimed in the First World War,' said the driver. 'Shell-shocked too. They gave him a pension – ten bob a week – but two years later he gave it up. They wanted him to go to London every year for an examination and he hated all the poking and pummelling. Must get on, though. I've got to be in Coventry by three.'

The engine started up, the lorry shuddered, and David had no time to say thank you before the driver set off in a cloud of smoke and fumes, a Christmas tune proclaiming peace and goodwill blaring from his radio.

The stars shone icily in the clear night sky – one, directly overhead, brighter than the rest. The grass verge was hard with frost. Shallow pools of ice had formed in the sunless shade and crackled now under David's shabby trainers. He fastened his thin anorak against the bone-chilling cold and limped unsteadily into the darkness.

Arriving at his uncle's farm, he searched in vain for the orchard, now covered by a large extension. New stables had been built and ornate brick paving replaced the uneven, muddy foldyard. A high curving brick wall – with letterbox and keypad for the wrought-iron gates – made the farm look like an army camp. The gates were open and the security lights flashed on, dazzling David as he squeezed between three cars and a horsebox. Nervously, he stroked the rough stubble on his pinched face and pressed the bell.

A young, olive-skinned man came to the door, his suit dark and expensive. 'How did you get in?' he said. 'The gates should be closed.'

'Do the Stephensons still live here?' asked David.

'What are you doing here?'

'I couldn't settle anywhere they found for me. I've just come from ...'

'I don't know anyone called Stephenson,' the young man interrupted him. 'We've only just moved in.'

David sank down on the doorstep, eyes glazed and expressionless.

'Are you alright? Would you like a glass of water or something?'

'Please,' said David. 'If you wouldn't mind.'

The young man returned with a glass and tried to wrap the cold, bony hand around it. To his horror, he saw that one of David's fingers was missing.

'It happened abroad,' said David. He tapped his head and smiled grimly. 'This too.'

Suddenly a shrill cry startled the two men. 'Joe, darling. Please come quickly. I think I've started. My contractions are shorter, my waters ... I knew we should have come home earlier. Elizabeth and I were both so excited, though. Our babies due the same day, and everything.'

'I'm sorry – you'll have to go,' Joe said to David. 'That's Mary.'

Joe's wife appeared at the door. 'Quick,' he continued, 'we'll take my car.' They made their way to the parked vehicles.

'No time,' gasped Mary, as a fresh spasm of pain shot through her body. 'The baby's coming now. Get me into the stables.'

David hadn't yet moved.

'Don't go,' Joe pleaded. 'Here, can you take her other arm?'

They found an empty stall and laid her down under a naked yellow light on a blanket in the straw.

Joe was panicking: 'I haven't a clue what to do,' he said.

David put his hand on the young man's shoulder to calm him. As a boy, he had often helped his uncle John deliver lambs in the old stables.

Mary was growing agitated, her body wracked by ever more frequent spasms of pain. David did his best to soothe her fears. He blew gently to warm his hands and placed them on her taut stomach. Her flesh felt clammy. Joe could hardly bring himself to look.

In the distance, the church clock in the village sounded its final midnight chime. Mary gave a long cry, an even longer shudder, and in the soft light of the stable her baby was born.

'A boy,' said David, 'a little boy.' Mary's child gave a gentle cry. David cupped the small head in his hand, trailing a finger lightly over a tiny, flawless hand.

Overcome with emotion, the two men were unable to speak. The scattered stars above no longer seemed quite so distant and cold, but shone like the light in Mary's eyes.

'Thank you,' said Joe with a nervous smile.

David took his small silver cross, each of its four straight arms decorated with a crown at the tip, and laid it gently beside the child. Mary reached out for it, turning it over to read the name and date on the reverse.

'David,' she murmured, 'a name for our son.'

'You must stay to rest,' said Joe. 'Have something to eat.'

'Yes, please stay,' said Mary.

'Just for this evening,' said David. 'Thank you.' He mustered a small smile. 'The cross is my gift to your child.' His mind and body were weary, but his heart was glad to have played a small part in the miracle of birth.

THOMAS CUTSFORTH

The Cutsforth family had lived in the same granite mansion overlooking Madeley, a hilly Pennine town of squat terraced houses, for three generations. For as long as anyone could remember, the family had owned iron foundries there. Later generations had diversified into cutlery manufacture, and in the post-war years Cutsforth foundries and steel mills had continued to ring the town like a tight metal band.

Thomas Cutsforth was sitting in his study examining figures. 'Profits down again,' he muttered. 'I'll have to close Shotley if this carries on.'

Thomas had last visited Shotley Foundry as a boy with his father when it was the jewel in the Cutsforth crown. The glow of molten metal speeding along narrow channels had excited him then, and still fascinated him now.

'I've finished with the tea-tray, Enid.'

His wife closed the thick curtains on the grey winter afternoon, then rattled coal from the brass scuttle onto the fire. Darkness temporarily cloaked the room.

'I've had a letter from my sister,' she said hesitantly from the shadows. 'She'd like us to stay next week.'

Thomas nodded briefly, glancing at his wife over his half-moon glasses, but then returned to his figures.

After Enid had departed, Thomas picked up the local paper. The front page featured some smiling charity workers holding a cheque, but he ignored them. Instead he scanned the share prices to see how his investments were doing, then he turned to the job advertisements: *Foundryman required. Shotley Foundry. 45-hour week*. A visit to his hard to please sister-in-law held no attraction, while a week at Shotley would give him plenty of time to identify the foundry's problems, shake the place up and make it profitable once again.

He'd go incognito, giving the address of a flat he owned in the neighbouring town; he'd be evasive about his P45 and National Insurance number, and he'd use his wife's maiden name. He was a solitary man – his only recreation the occasional fishing trip to the Yorkshire coast – and he was unlikely to be recognised. He'd recently been mistaken for a visitor in his own office. He rarely went to Shotley Foundry – far away at the other end of the valley – and its manager Harry Westby was in hospital. He'd turn up ill shaven on his first day and let his stubble grow into a beard.

*   *   *   *

In the cold half-light of morning Thomas tramped through powdery snow to the tram terminus far above the town. His mansion – Cutsforth's Hermitage, some called it sardonically – lay higher still, amid ice-rimmed birch and larch trees. Thomas felt strangely elated by his deception. The tram slid between houses transformed by the light overnight snowfall. Occasionally it groaned to a stop for a group of solemn, sleepy workers – an icy blast piercing the carriage every time the sliding door jerked open. Then the bell rang, the tram jolted forward, and the workers inside returned to their newspapers or their thoughts.

Thomas stroked the thick stubble on his chin, pulled his greasy cap low over his eyes and peered at the valley below. The canal – normally disfigured by dirty, foaming waste – was covered now with glassy white ice. Smoke from his foundries drifted across the pale sky like mountainous floes of polar ice.

'You look a bit lost, mate,' said the Shotley gateman. The day had remained overcast, with slanting needles of sleet, and the snow around the foundry gates was muddy slush.

'I'm starting here today,' said Thomas.

'You'd better see Charlie, then.' The gateman stroked his unshaven chin and looked at his pocket watch. 'Ted's the foreman, but he won't be in today. He'll be at Holy Cross in a couple of hours or so.'

'What for?' asked Thomas.

'A funeral.' The gateman smiled grimly. 'Our boss, Harry Westby.'

Thomas had known Harry all his life: they'd played football together as boys. Harry had been a centre-half, a genial giant of a man with a wry sense of humour.

A stifling wall of heat confronted Thomas as he entered the foundry. Blue flames sparked in the farthest corner, and two buckets full of molten metal dangled from the roof. Charlie led him into a mess room and came to a halt in front of a shabby green locker, door hanging off on one hinge. 'Here,' he said. 'You can have this one.' Then he turned to some shower cubicles, their tiles cracked and dirty. 'There are showers too if you want. And you'll need some protective clothing, I suppose. I'm not sure we've any metal-capped boots your size, though.'

'Who's the lad with one arm?' Thomas asked later as they walked through the foundry together.

'That's Jack Rawlings. He had an accident on the strip-cutting saw last year. Harry kept him on. Head Office doesn't know though. He sweeps up and runs errands. That's all he's fit for now. We asked for a new guard for the saw. Cutsforth's lad was dealing with it, but they've lost the paperwork somewhere along the line. Apparently Young Cutsforth spends most of his time jaunting round Europe on expenses.'

Thomas started at the sound of his son's name.

Layers of white dust covered the floors and machinery. Thomas's throat felt dry and he started to cough. 'New delivery of limestone,' said Charlie, eyebrows frosted like the crags under winter snow. 'You'll soon get used to it. It finds its way into everything.'

Thomas looked at his watch. At Head Office he'd be dealing with his post by now and listening for the rattle of the tea-trolley. Mrs Gibbons would talk even though he was busy, producing photos of her grandchildren, holiday snaps of her and Mr Gibbons happy and relaxed on the prom at Torquay, or pictures of the new conservatory with its expensive pine furniture.

Two men covered in dust and grease were just emerging from a narrow aperture in one of the furnaces. 'That's the Queen Mary,' said Charlie. 'We're doing some maintenance work on it.' He pointed to a metal barrow and a shovel. 'I want you to help move the slurry to the dump outside.'

Thomas lowered himself in and started shovelling up waste and slurry. It was dark and hot inside the furnace, freezing outside in the sharp winter air.

'Where does all this stuff go?' he asked one of the lorry-drivers.

'To Shotley Quarry. There's a hole the size of Wembley Stadium. Everything goes in, including these metal drums.'

At lunchtime, Thomas joined the other workers in the small recess of a loading bay. Shoulders hunched, they unfastened their snap-tins full of thick sandwiches.

He tried to chat to another of the men cleaning out the furnace but he found it very difficult.

'Deaf,' mouthed a third man. 'He used to work in the reeling section. Very noisy, machines going all day.'

One young man sat quietly sketching – prompting Thomas to recall that drawings had covered one of the mess-room walls. The artist quickly completed a caricature of Thomas and handed it to him. One o'clock already. Ann Saltonstall would be serving poached salmon in the directors' restaurant right now. Thomas pictured her pleasant smile as she skilfully scooped fish onto his large white plate. A tall girl, her uniform always clean and freshly ironed, Ann had not gone unnoticed by Enid Cutsforth, who had also been quick to employ her as a cleaner for a few hours a week.

*   *   *   *

In mid-afternoon an ambulance arrived from Madeley Royal Infirmary: Thomas had collapsed inside the furnace. 'Poor old blighter,' said Charlie to the driver. 'He only started here this morning. They usually last a bit longer than that.'

'Your name?' asked the nurse when they arrived in Casualty.

'Thomas Cutsforth.'

The nurse smiled in disbelief, wrinkling her turned-up nose at his greasy cap, shabby overalls and grey stubble.

Thomas suddenly remembered that although his name might be quite well known in town, his face was not.

'It says here you're called Thomas Deighton,' she said.

'That's my wife's maiden name,' replied Thomas, sighing wearily and closing his eyes. He felt very tired. Who could he call? He couldn't send for Peter and his icy spendthrift of a daughter-in-law. 'Here,' he said, 'ring this number and ask for Ann Saltonstall in the staff restaurant. Ask her to come here straight away.'

Thomas closed his eyes again.

A short time later he heard Ann's voice: 'Well, Mr Cutsforth, I am sorry to see you like this.'

'Take my house key, Ann,' he said. 'Light fires in the dining-room and my study, would you? And could you cook a meal for me this evening? My wife's spending the week with her sister in Southport. I don't want news of this getting any further.' He pointed meaningfully towards his overalls, seeking the approval of the young nurse. 'I'm feeling better already. I think I'm ready to be discharged.'

'Yes, Mr Cutsforth,' Ann replied, gathering up his dirty clothes.

*   *   *   *

A fire blazed in the hearth. A bank of black clouds rose above the crags, a rose-petal glow threatening heavy snow by nightfall. Light from the room illuminated smooth drifts among the bare trees. Deer were out there on the moors: Thomas imagined them sheltering in a hollow, their wet noses nuzzling the frozen heather.

He folded his newspaper as Ann brought in a couple of plates. 'I enjoyed your singing,' he said. He'd been listening to her while she worked in the kitchen. He wanted to go on and tell her how it made the house seem lived in. Dustsheets covered much of their furniture; heavy curtains in every room remained permanently drawn. Every day Enid came into his study to dust before moving on quickly to complete a close inspection of the entire house, brushing the curtains as she went.

Ann smiled shyly, smoothing her overall down with her hands before taking it off and folding it carefully. They sat together quietly, warmed by the flames of the fire.

Thomas paused, smiling unexpectedly when he removed a crumpled sheet of paper from his pocket.

'It's one of John Marritt's,' said Ann, glancing at the caricature. This time her smile was less reserved, moving all the way to her eyes.

Thomas studied Ann's small, womanly features. Her arms were thin, one wrist encircled by an engraved, loose-fitting bracelet – her long fingers sometimes sought it out like a rosary. A few early lines of tiredness around her fine eyes only added to her beauty when she smiled.

'I'm going to sell this house,' he said suddenly. 'Close down Shotley Foundry.'

'Money and possessions certainly can blind a person, Thomas.'

Thomas looked up, slightly nettled by her remark. 'Like a pauper in the sight of God,' he said.

Ann looked puzzled.

'It's from the Bible,' said Thomas. 'It describes a wealthy man.'

He knew he was losing count of all his bank accounts and investments. Only the other day he'd come across some long-forgotten stock certificates and fretted about his oversight for days afterwards. And he despaired at the thought of his daughter-in-law's extravagance.

Nonetheless he smiled: it was the first time Ann had called him Thomas.

He knew something of Ann's background from Enid. She had been widowed in the last weeks of the war, a telegram bringing bad news when she'd been expecting good. Her husband had been a prisoner-of-war and had died on the long forced winter march from his camp in the east to Hamburg. Ann was now in her early forties and had never remarried, remaining instead with her mother. The name of her father was inscribed on Madeley's war memorial. He'd been sent home from France with a raging mouth abscess, declared fit almost immediately and, still in great pain, returned to the Somme, where he was killed a couple of days later.

Thomas turned his thoughts back to Shotley. He'd hardly ever visited the place before today, content to share in the foundry's profits year after year and leave his son to run it. The conditions had been dirty and dangerous. He'd seen strange, mole-like blotches on the faces and forearms of many of those who worked near the heat of the furnaces. Men like Harry Westby died before their time.

Thomas tried to still his troubled mind. How often had he passed Harry in town with no more than a brief nod? He cleared his throat. 'I'm going to arrange a pension for Harry Westby's widow,' he said.

'You must go and see her, Thomas,' said Ann, moving closer and kneeling by his armchair. Her curly dark hair was swept back girlishly, gathered with a simple ribbon in the nape of her neck. 'And there are others at the foundry you mustn't forget.'

Thomas nodded. 'Yes, the boy with one arm and the deaf man in the loading bay.'

'There's Heather as well.' Ann glanced at a photograph of Thomas's daughter surrounded by a group of African children. 'She might like you to visit her.'

'I'll send her some money for one of her schemes. She's always writing to tell me how desperately they need clean water and malaria nets.'

He paused then to consider his son. It was time the auditors examined the cost of all Peter's trips abroad. Father and son had argued the last time they met. Peter's daughter was there at the time, thrashing around on her bed during one of her frequent fits – body stiffening, limbs flailing, eyes flickering and rolling. Thomas found it agony to watch his only grandchild and rarely visited his son at home.

Food and rest had brought the colour back to Thomas's face. 'I should leave now,' said Ann. The two of them tried to open the front door, but the cold easterly wind had brought a blizzard with it, creating deep drifts and almost sealing the door shut. The only movement came from the large, swirling snowflakes. The wind moaned gently. The branch of a tree, heavy with snow, brushed against a window.

'I never liked disturbing freshly fallen snow when I was a child,' said Ann, eyes bright with anticipation. 'I longed for it to come and I was always so sad when it thawed and the town turned dull and misty.'

She turned to face him.

'There's something I must tell you before I go. I went over to Shotley a few weeks ago to prepare a retirement tea for one of the managers. John Marritt saw me and sketched me. I've been out with him a few times since. He's a bit younger than me, and I like him very much. He's asked me to marry him.'

Thomas went over to his writing-cabinet and took out his cheque-book. 'Please accept this gift for your wedding expenses.'

'My grandfather owned a small chemist's shop,' said Ann, growing serious once more. 'He always remembered gifts for Christmas and birthdays, and always included a poem or saying he thought might help us in our lives, carefully written in his flowing hand. I've kept them all. I looked forward to them more than the gifts.' Ann shivered as she handed back the cheque.

Thomas sighed and closed his eyes. For all his riches he'd become a lonely, troubled man. Just then a notion sprang into his head. He would renounce his wealth – it was no more to him now than the dross in one of his furnaces. He would abandon his old life, give away this Victorian house – dreary even on the sunniest of days – where generations of Cutsforths, himself included, had lived in stony indifference to the rest of the world. He would rip down the heavy curtains that Enid brushed so obsessively.

The house could become a centre where young people from the back streets could come and explore the countryside. More ideas came to him. He'd resign as Managing Director and stand for election to the local council. His foundries had scarred the local area – he'd try and clean up the valley. He'd ask Heather to bring over a group of African children. There would be musical events for Enid, and charity fund-raisers for disabled children like his grand-daughter. Thomas felt as elated as earlier in the day when he had tramped through the powdery snow to catch the tram for Shotley Foundry.

Closeted from the outside world on that dark winter night, Thomas slipped into sleep. Ann Saltonstall moved a little closer and lightly kissed a face so often, but now no longer, set in a frown.

SHEBA

'That was Mother on the phone,' Katherine said to her younger sister Caitlin. 'Apparently the concert finishes at nine-thirty, not eight-thirty.'

'Did you tell her ice-hockey training starts at nine?' asked Caitlin.

'Oh no, I forgot. And I can't ring back. She was calling from a phone box and they'll be in the concert hall by now. She also told us not to feed Sheba. She's got something special for her later on.'

'Sheba'll be hungry by then. And what about Keith? He's only ten and he'll be on his own if we go to ice hockey. Except for Sheba – but a cat's not like having a dog in the house.'

The aging Sheba rose slowly at the mention of her name, stretching, yawning and arching her back. Then she settled down again sleepily in her domain on the rug in front of the gas fire. Only now was the cat beginning to feel at home after the Kenningtons' move to this large, four-storey Georgian house in Hammersmith.

'Let's go to ice hockey,' said Katherine. 'Keith'll be fine. He'll only be on his own for half an hour or so before they get back. We'd better take an umbrella though. There's rain forecast.'

The girls picked an umbrella from the stand in the hall, where their father Alan also kept the walking sticks he collected on holiday in the Alps.

'Where are the hockey-sticks?' asked Caitlin.

'Just behind the basement door,' replied Katherine. 'Top of the stairs.' The basement was gloomy and still unfurnished. Rats had been found down there and their father wanted to get rid of them before he tackled it.

The two girls left the house, leaving Keith alone with Sheba. His mother Pamela cradled the purring creature as if it was a baby, her long red fingernails ruffling its black fur. 'Cats don't like changing houses,' she would say to him. 'They find it difficult to adjust. You've got to be really sensitive towards them for the first few months.'

Pamela didn't seem to care that her son had moved to a different school and found it hard to make new friends. When she arrived home from the concert, Keith knew she would look first for Sheba. Only the other day he'd disturbed his mother in her black leotard, almond-shaped eyes set above high cheekbones, arching her back and stretching like a cat. 'Sorry,' he'd muttered, and run away.

Watchful, solitary on the rug in front of the fire, Sheba blinked in the gathering gloom. Keith too closed his eyes and drowsed. Suddenly the cat startled him awake. Sheba shrieked and howled, toppling ornaments as she raced dementedly around the room. Keith grabbed one of his father's sticks to defend himself, wounding the cat as he lashed out again and again. Eventually, she gasped her final breath and fell dead with a thud like an old, worn-out sack.

Keith could scarcely bear to stroke Sheba when she was alive: dead, he had to remove her quickly from his sight. The basement door was open so he just shovelled her behind it.

*   *   *   *

'What on earth has happened here?' asked Pamela Kennington, gazing in horror

40

at the wreckage of the room. 'Where's my Sheba?'

'Behind the door,' muttered Keith.

'Which door?' asked his father.

'The basement.' Keith began to sob.

Pamela howled in anguish when she found the furry heap.

Her husband was puzzled. 'She's got traces of food around her whiskers.'

'But I asked the girls not to feed her,' said Pamela. 'I made a special salmon dinner for her to eat later. And why was the basement door open?'

The couple walked down the uncarpeted steps together. Face flushed, Alan fidgeted uncomfortably.

Pamela flicked on the basement light. A bowl stood on the dusty floorboards, illuminated by a single, naked bulb. 'That's one of Sheba's bowls,' she said accusingly. 'What's it doing down here?'.

'It's for the rats,' replied Alan. 'There are so many bowls in the kitchen with Sheba's name on them. I couldn't find any others to ... ' His voice trailed off feebly into the darkness.

'Aaagh,' shrieked Pamela.

Keith stood at the top of the stairs. No one had yet met his eyes. Slowly he turned and made his way up to his room.

THE FLAWED PLATE

'It's John, isn't it?' asked Leonard Yardley, returning his portly form to the leather armchair and smoothing down the sharp creases of his trousers. He'd dressed and washed in a hurry: a thin layer of pottery dust gathered in the creases around his eyes when he turned a wintry smile on the young man.

A few weeks earlier John Heathrington had returned home to 24 Gladstone Street to find a stranger in the front room. His mother had lowered her eyes in embarrassment when John came in. 'Leonard, I mean Mr Yardley, is going to install some lights for us,' she said.

Now Yardley was jabbering on at him. 'Your mother mentioned you'd taken up watercolour painting.'

John nodded.

'If you're as talented as Rona, it could lead to a job in the pottery now you've left school.' Yardley coughed, spluttering into his handkerchief.

'I may have other plans,' John replied.

'Other plans, my word! When I was just a bit older than you I was caught up in the war, rewiring aerodromes and servicing planes every hour of the day and night.' Yardley thrust his thick red hands upwards. 'Brains in these,' he bragged.

Yardley was getting excited and his cough came back with a vengeance. 'Anyway,' he continued, impatiently, 'I've asked your mother to marry me.'

'Really,' said John. 'Is that all you've got to say?'

'No, I'll have a drink too, something to stop this cough. Go and talk things over with your mother. She can have a sherry to celebrate. And you can have a shandy – no harm in that. Cheer up. For the first time you'll have a real father.'

Anger coursed through John's veins.

'Sorry about that,' said Yardley, settling back and caressing the shiny leather armchair as if it already belonged to him. The room was threadbare and cold, undisturbed since the time of Rona's parents. He'd try and make some changes to please her.

'There's whisky, ' said John, opening the sideboard and placing a bottle on the table.

Yardley hesitated: the whisky somehow gave the drab room a translucent, golden glow. 'No, no, I'm on shift later. I'll settle for a cup of tea with your mother when the two of you have finished.'

*   *   *   *

Rona Heathrington was a tall woman, fresh of complexion and still attractive, despite the hint of hardness now apparent around her clear blue eyes. She was sitting in the kitchen with Uncle Harold and placed her sewing on her lap when her son came into the room.

'Is Leonard alright?' she asked.

An edgy silence took hold.

'He's after a drink,' said John.

His mother looked anxiously at the door.

'Only a cup of tea,' he continued.

'I must have been dozing while you and Leonard were talking.' Rona smiled

42

faintly to herself as water drummed into the kettle. 'Supper's on the table.'

'That clock's stopped again,' said John. He'd tinkered with it earlier and been happy to get it going.

'I'll ask Leonard to have a look ...' She coloured up. 'You don't mind that he's asking me to marry him,' she said quickly.

'You can't, Mother.'

'Why?'

'Something about him isn't right,' John said moodily.

'He's good at his job,' said Rona. 'Everyone in the factory goes to him when things break down. The other women say he's always helpful.'

'You've not handed any money over, have you?' asked John. One of his aunts was always falling in love and had foolishly presented her fiancé with all her savings a week before the wedding was due.

Next door, the coughing had ceased temporarily: now all they could hear were snores. John put a cup of tea on a tray for Leonard. 'Leave him be,' said Rona. 'Let's talk. I'm thirty-five, and now the war's over I want to move out of the shadows a bit. You don't want me to end up cold, frail and alone like a First World War widow,do you?'

'We can manage without Yardley's money,' said John. 'I'm hoping to start work this year. There's your wages from the factory. The house belongs to us ... well, to you and Uncle Harold. I don't like Yardley. We don't need to depend on him.'

'We have to depend every day on people we don't like,' said Rona.

'We don't have live with them, though,' replied John.

He sat down heavily on the arm of his mother's chair and placed his hand on her shoulder. Meanwhile Uncle Harold stirred. Hunched and gasping, expression blank, the old soldier stared straight ahead. His life had effectively come to an end at the battle of the Somme.

'Leonard will be able to help with Harold,' Rona pleaded. 'He's going to bring his daughter with him next time he comes.'

'He's been married before, then?'

'His wife left him. She met a GI at the end of the war and they went off to America. Leonard was very upset.'

'I'm sure he was,' said John.

Rona picked up the plate she'd used for John's sandwiches. 'Do you know, this is the first thing I ever painted in the factory,' she said, smiling. She ran her hand over the raised leaves and orchids around the edge. 'I thought it was perfect, but it wasn't. Frank Dixon inspected all the work in those days. I can see him now in his worn brown overall. He never missed a fault. His brush strokes were so quick and accurate. He'd lean over you, pick up the brush, and paint the pattern in a flash. The girls used to giggle about him. He always had an unlit cigarette dangling from his mouth and some of them said they'd even seen it in there while he was eating his sandwiches.'

'You can't tell the plate's flawed,' said John. 'It's very good for a first attempt.'

'I looked for it afterwards and found it in the factory shop where they sold seconds,' continued Rona. 'That's when I was going out with your father.'

'Tell me more about him,' said John, forgetting all about Leonard Yardley, fast asleep in the next room.

'Your father had many interests,' said Rona, putting the plate down by the sink. 'Science fascinated him; he liked literature and music, and he could paint. His family had been in the army for generations. It was always his ambition to join the guards. He was tall, like you, and fair. Somehow, he couldn't settle around here.'

'Did he join up?' asked John.

'Yes, he disappeared suddenly and went off to join the Grenadier Guards in London. Shortly afterwards I found I was expecting you. He came back and wanted to marry me, but my parents wouldn't agree to it. They thought I'd been disgraced. We used to meet in one of those alleyways at the top of the street. There was talk of a mother and baby home – of adoption. I suppose I should have been stronger.'

Yardley's gravelly cough sounded from next door.

'He'll have to get rid of that before the wedding,' said Rona. 'Leonard hasn't taken very good care of his health.'

*   *   *   *

A few days later Leonard Yardley moved into the spare room in the attic. John was often aware of low voices at bedtime, but for the most part he could hear nothing but Yardley's persistent cough.

One evening John returned home from night school to find his mother's face bruised and the sewing table broken.

'What happened?' he asked. 'Where's Leonard?'

'I stumbled, fell on the taps,' said Rona. 'No, no, that's not true.'

The fire had burned low and the house was cold.

'Leonard wouldn't stop coughing. It just went on and on. I had to do something about it with the wedding so near, so I made him a hot drink.'

John looked puzzled.

'That's not all. I added a good splash of whisky. He demanded more, gulping it wildly from the bottle. Then suddenly he turned violent.' Rona waved her arm in the direction of the broken sewing table. 'There's something else too'

'What?' asked John, picking up the broken table.

She paused, tears trickling down her cheek.

'I can't forgive him. I could never forgive him – he smashed my plate while we were struggling.'

'The one you painted when you first started at the pottery.'

'Yes,' said Rona quietly. 'He has a problem with drink, doesn't he? Leonard Yardley won't be coming back.'

'Flawed, like your plate,' said her son, picking up the empty bottle and throwing it in the bin.

A BATT OUT OF HELL

'I'm going away,' said Charlie Batt, managing director of Charles Batt Luxury Kitchen (UK) Ltd.

'We're all really sorry, Boss,' said Ernie Loftus, nodding to two of his colleagues. 'That's if you're going to be banged up again.' Rumours had been rife in the factory: the auditors had found boxes of bank-notes in one of the store-rooms during stocktaking.

'We'll visit you, though' purred Tracey Feasey from Customer Care, Teasy Feasey to those on the factory floor. She reached over and patted Charlie's tattooed forearm. 'We'll bring you a few home comforts too.' She fluttered her heavily lacquered false eyelashes at Charlie just as she had before he passed her over for Sharon in Despatch.

'Visits? Banged up?' Charlie was puzzled. His eagle eyes roved around the table.

'He's going to make an honest woman of Angela – at last.' Tracey was excited. Angela was Charlie Batt's long-suffering and heavily pregnant girlfriend. Perhaps the factory-girls could have a hen night on the town. 'That's why you're going away.'

'And you're going to do the honourable thing for the child,' concluded Leeroy Walsh from Packaging, his black skin gleaming like the ebony worktop of a Batt kitchen.

'They're not banging me up and I'm not going to do the honourable thing by Angie,' shouted Charlie Batt. He banged his fist hard on the table. 'Not going to prison, not prepared to tie the matrimonial knot. Understand.'

'But what about the money they found in the warehouse, Boss?' persisted Ernie.

'Sponsorship money from the London Marathon,' replied Charlie, unbuttoning his shirt to show the 1995 medallion nestling on his hairy chest.

'But the Marathon, that was five years ago,' said Leeroy. He was still bitter about the cash Charlie had snatched from his pay packet at the time.

'A few alterations here and there,' smirked Charlie. 'That was all it took to satisfy the auditors – and they gave me a ten-quid note.' Charlie waved the letter he held in his hand. 'However, the Inland Revenue and my accountants have suggested I could do with some training. Apparently I have to know all about graaphs, BAACS payments and long term financial plaans.' Charlie imitated the long vowels of the elegantly dressed, sweetly perfumed lady sent to persuade him of the need for training. Hilary Barrington had exerted plenty of pressure. Charlie did his best to resist but changed his mind when told she was running the course.

'How long will you be gone for?' asked Ernie. The idea of a custodial sentence for his boss still had plenty of appeal.

'Five days,' said Charlie. 'So no thieving while I'm away. Or any late night deals on Ilkley Moor.'

'Ilkley Moor,' echoed Tracey, eyes dreamy.

'Don't worry, Boss,' said Leeroy. 'We'll take care of the factory while you're away.'

'See that worktop over there,' said Charlie. 'It reminds me of you lot. It's thick. Batt quality, mind you, but still thick. You can't think for yourselves, no initiative.'

*　　*　　*　　*

Not an hour after Charlie had climbed into his twin-exhaust BMW and left for his management course in Croydon, the factory was like a ship becalmed. His workers were noticeably less jumpy. They smiled and exchanged pleasantries with customers; they even apologised for their mistakes.

Ernie Loftus had already made himself at home in Charlie Batt's office. He swivelled round in the black leather executive chair. 'Remember,' he said to Leeroy Walsh. 'Charlie told us to think for ourselves, use our initiative.'

'He told us no thieving and no deals.'

'We've still got to do all we can to protect the factory from break-ins. My brother-in-law supplies close-circuit security equipment – cameras, that sort of thing. He'd set them up here and throw in a few DVD recorders and tellys as part of the deal.'

'Flat-screen tellys?' asked Leeroy, remembering the nightly bashing that kept his old set in focus.

'Yes, big, big screens,' replied Ernie and reached for the order book.

*　　*　　*　　*

The break-in took place the evening before Charlie's return from Croydon.

'There's always the insurance,' said Ernie at the next office meeting.

'Haven't paid the premiums,' snapped Charlie. He'd enjoyed no luck with stuck-up Hilary Barrington. 'Place is crawling with coppers – any excuse to snoop around.' He twitched when he recognised two plain-clothes officers behind the glass office doors.

'Coffee?' Tracey asked the policemen.

'Do you have a DVD recorder, Mr Batt?' said the older of the two. 'These pictures appeared on your security cameras.'

'Security cameras, what security cameras?' snarled Charlie, as a shifty figure in a 1995 London Marathon T-shirt appeared on screen, removed a load of cash from a box hidden underneath some kitchen units and hopped over the low factory wall.

'Very athletic, Mr Batt. In training for the Great North Run, are we, sir? I understand the tax office is looking for some sponsorship.'

THE CROSS

'An unusual name,' said Alfred Mendoza, scanning the label on the manila folder in front of him and thumbing lazily through a few notes and papers.

'Yes, it's Polish,' said Paul Leskiewicz. 'My parents came over to England as children after the war.' The young man glanced at the badge on the lapel of Mendoza's grey pin-striped suit. 'And your name?'

'Spanish, I believe, somewhere back in time.' Mendoza looked up from his notes. 'But I'm an Englishman just like you.'

The two men exchanged polite smiles.

Paul ran his hand anxiously through his fair hair. The vast, fiery ball of the sun was beginning to drop in a cloudless blue sky – just as it had that evening in France. The details were still vivid in his mind. Driving to Spain, in searing heat, he'd broken his journey at an old fortified hill town – its squat white buildings interspersed with dark cypress trees.

Paul unclenched his fingers and wiped his warm, moist hands on his handkerchief. The empty, tree-lined streets had been oppressively silent. Solid, château-like buildings of dark stone surrounded the town square, the shadows of the military heroes on their marble plinths growing ever longer in the evening light. Occasionally, a clock had chimed, softly, in the windless, stifling air.

Mendoza drew the blind to block out the early evening sun and turned to pour his patient a glass of water. 'We need to dig deeper to get to the bottom of this,' he said. 'It's not an uncommon experience. You were in a strange place and tired after travelling all day.' His brown eyes grew softer under their heavy Spanish lids. 'Let's go through it all again.'

Paul lowered his gaze and started to speak – uncertainly at first, as if ashamed. 'We walked through the town centre, then climbed steadily up a narrow, winding road with high, dark walls and overhanging trees on either side. We came round a bend and suddenly we were out on the open hillside. A broad, shimmering plain stretched out in front of us for mile after mile. The sun was sinking and everything was absolutely still. The hills round about were covered in squat, whitewashed houses that seemed in danger of tumbling down to the plain below.'

Paul stopped, his heart pounding.

Mendoza leaned forward intently. 'Go on.'

'There was a large cross on top of one of the hills, standing out against the fading, pinkish-blue light. It looked black and starkly beautiful.'

'And what happened next?' urged the doctor.

'I panicked. I felt that I was clinging onto the edge of a world spinning out of control. The setting sun disappeared in a molten glow. Space seemed indifferent, cold and empty.'

'Can you remember exactly when that sensation took hold?' asked Mendoza, his gaze intelligent and steady.

'It was the cross,' said Paul. 'That's what made me feel uneasy.' His brain had drummed as if desperate to burst free of his skull. 'My family's Catholic. The sight of a cross shouldn't affect me like that, should it?'

'Is this the only time you've experienced such feelings?' asked Mendoza, refilling his patient's glass.

'No,' said Paul. 'It happened again just recently, at a cricket match. I'd forgotten all about the incident in France. The scores were just drawing level when the setting sun flashed on the pavilion windows. I panicked again. I had to run for cover to the pub next door.'

'The sun has been rising and setting for millions of years.' Mendoza waved his hand expansively. 'You must think about this rationally, confront your fears. Sunsets are beautiful, uplifting spectacles.'

He paused and looked directly at the young man. 'Return to that town. Return and visit that cross.'

*　*　*　*

Paul Leskiewicz travelled again to France. This time it was midday, the sun high in the sky, when he stood on the hillside looking out on that broad plain. People were out and about, tourists with their comforting, friendly chatter. He'd passed a noisy, open-air market, its stalls piled high with colourful fruit and vegetables. He fixed his eyes on the dark cross, its outline sharper than before.

He went to enquire in the local bus station. 'The village with the large black cross,' he said. 'I'd like to visit it.'

An hour later he was standing beneath the cross itself. Constructed from a solid block of stone, it bore an inscription followed by a list of names and ages.

An aeroplane had crashed into this hillside during the Second World War. Paul's eyes moved slowly down the names: Anton Leskiewicz – aged thirty-six – Polish Squadron – Royal Air Force. It was his grandfather.

ELVIRAS

'I just opened today,' said Elviras brightly. She patted her dark, shoulder-length hair. It fell loosely in curls as if it had just been washed but hadn't yet fully dried.

An athletic young man in running shorts was standing on the opposite side of the café counter: 'In time for the start of the season?'

'Yes, that's right.'

She poured milk into a jug, a smile seemingly never far from her speckled-blue eyes.

The wooden hut lay on a cliff track: it was raised on railway sleepers and offered balcony chairs and tables for passing walkers. Neil would stop there during his runs to check his pulse and complete a few stretching exercises, or to shelter from the rain. A long flight of wooden steps led from the track down to the beach.

'My father's Spanish, from Catalonia,' said Elviras. 'He only stayed in this country a couple of years. I think the winters drove him away. My mother's English though. They met when she was on holiday. He was a hotel waiter in San Sebastian. I'm Elviras, Elviras Idoa Lasa.'

'I'm Neil. I'm in training for a cross-country race, regional level.'

'Would you like a drink?' Elviras smiled. Her teeth were white, neat and even.

'No thanks,' said Neil. 'I only drink filtered water.' He completed a stretching routine and moved to the door. 'Anyway, I must be going.'

Dreamily, Elviras watched him run back along the sloping track into town, his long legs moving as smoothly as pistons. She limped out from behind the counter and sat down. There were still no customers about: Neil didn't really count. Her specially made left boot felt uncomfortable and she eased it off slowly to rub her foot. Her mother had once altered the hem of a dress, lengthening it on one side to cover her foot.

Elviras was normally even tempered, but a wave of anger suddenly overcame her – a longing to be like others, maybe even to run like Neil. She sighed, taking a strange kind of comfort from the advancing tide that now covered the sands below.

*   *   *   *

A couple of days later Elviras watched again as Neil ran up the flinty track.

'Training going well?' she asked.

'I've a blister on my heel. These new running shoes have been a big disappointment.'

She picked up a filter jug and poured him a glass of water.

'You remembered my filtered water.'

'I've not had that many customers.'

'You need to advertise,' said Neil, pointing towards the town. 'And you need a better sign. Come outside and I'll show you where to fix it. The hut needs sprucing up at bit as well.'

Elviras remained behind the counter.

'Show me some other time. I've stock to check in the freezer. Things may be busier today.'

'I should be going anyway,' said Neil, glancing at his training watch. 'Thanks for the water.'

Some weeks later, Neil, still tense and angry after a poor result in the cross-country, arrived at the café to find a 'To Let' board outside. A skylark hovered above the yellow gorse and warbled its piercing song. Meanwhile the café sign was flapping in the wind, shabbier than ever.

Back in town, Neil called into the estate agent's office. He spoke to a female assistant and pointed out the photograph of the café among the properties to let.

'Oh, that one.' said the woman, flicking through the file with her long fingernails. 'The girl only came in the other day to give notice.'

'Did she say why?' asked Neil.

'She was finding it too much, I suppose. Her foot must have made things difficult for her.'

'Foot?' said Neil. 'What do you mean, foot?'

'She was lame. She had a special boot. Pretty little thing, with blue eyes.'

'Like a skylark's egg,' murmured Neil.

*　　*　　*　　*

Later, Neil found himself outside a small terrace house.

Elviras opened the door.

'I didn't realise you were ...' said Neil.

'Lame with a made-up boot.'

'Was it hurting the day I called in?'

'Uncomfortable maybe – it's often like that.'

'But you were always smiling whenever I came by.'

'I laugh easily and sometimes I cry just as easily,' said Elviras. 'It must be something to do with my Spanish temperament.' She paused. 'How did you do in the cross-country?'

'I got an injury halfway through the race,' said Neil, gazing down in embarrassment. How could he say a blister had forced him to retire? He thought of the impassive faces of those self-absorbed girls in the gym who rarely spoke or smiled. 'Take on the café again,' he said. 'I'll help you.'

'Will you now? And why would you do that?'

Neil grinned. 'Let's just say it's your speckled-blue eyes.'

*　　*　　*　　*

The weather changed. No longer shrouded in grey sea mist, the towering chalk stacks on the island across the bay flashed white in the strong sunlight. The eternal ring of children's voices at play mingled with the muffled sound of a summer sea growing sleepy as it repeatedly washed over sand and shingle. Armed with a box of sandwiches and a drink, Neil jogged up and down the wooden steps leading to the beach.

That evening the moon cast a shimmering bar of light on the dark sea, and on a freshly painted sign: Elviras'.

VINCENT

Hagen and his companion stood in the lighted window of the upstairs room.

'He's just gone,' said Hagen.

'Who?'

'Vincent, that artist fellow. His pictures look like a messy palette – depressing things, all heavy daubing, dark blues and greys. He flew at me in a rage when I said he must have put the paint on the canvas with his hands. Splashes it all over the floor and stains the walls with palette-knife scrapings: he just doesn't care. When I told him to paint in the grounds, I never expected he'd be out there at night painting the sky.'

'Where's he going to stay?'

'There's a woman in town with a child: Vincent thinks it's his, calls him *his little boy*. He says he's going to stay with her.'

Vincent was still outside on a gravel path, staring up at the pair. His eyes were like those of an eagle, a piercing china blue. He scattered the tablets Hagen had given him, picked up a rucksack and slung it over his narrow shoulders. Although a youngish man, his ginger beard was already flecked with grey. His face was thin, wasted and angular, the skin stretched tightly over his cheekbones like the unfinished canvas on his back. He shivered in his thin anorak and pulled a hat edged with matted fur over his shaven head and bandage-covered ear.

The cypresses in the grounds towered against the indigo sky as Vincent stumbled along a path shaded by a laurel hedge. He cursed as a thorn scratched his hand when he stumbled and fell into the shrubs.

Out on the road, his fast, ungainly gait soon brought him to a tenement close by a sluggish canal. Vincent hammered on the front door with both hands.

'Christine! Christine!' he shouted, his voice growing louder and more agitated.

A light came on in a bedroom, and shortly afterwards a woman appeared at the door, shoulders fleshy white above her dressing-gown, her voice like the yelp of a pup. 'Go away,' she said. 'You disgust me.' She lit a cigarette, inhaling deeply.

'Where's our boy?'

'He's with his father.'

'But I'm his father. He's *my* son. I pay the rent on this house. If it wasn't for me you'd be out on the streets.' When Vincent was painting, the boy would tug at his coat until he took him on his lap. They'd talk about plants, animals and birds. Vincent had once painted a picture for the boy's room – an orchard clad in pink and white blossom, bathed in sunlight.

A male voice sounded from inside the house: 'Are you coming?'

Vincent clenched his knuckles and bit down hard. Smash it against the door, said the voice in his head: more pain that way.

'I told you to keep away', said Christine, tossing her tousled hair.

Vincent had picked her up in the docklands and asked her to model for him. She was tall with broad child-bearing hips, but neither particularly young or especially beautiful. She had both attracted and repulsed him. He'd felt sorry for her: life had not treated her kindly.

Vincent felt for the bandage covering his ear. He had found his friend Garrigan in bed with Christine and fought with him. Then he had severed his own earlobe and presented it to her. In return Garrigan had presented Vincent with Garrigan's own painting of the woman.

'My drawing!' pleaded Vincent, the lines on his forehead ever more deeply etched. 'My paintings! What have you done with them?'

'They're in the backyard with the rest of the rubbish,' shrieked Christine, and the door closed on an odour of dust, alcohol and tobacco.

In the yard, Vincent picked up a nude study of Christine crouching in despair. He rolled it up carefully and placed it in his rucksack alongside his brushes and paints. He'd agonised over this drawing, been pleased with it. At last, he thought, he'd found his muse.

His anger passed. He'd never had much success with women. He wandered to the bottom of the street and stumbled into a public house. It was crowded, noisy with music and drunken singing.

Vincent unhitched his easel and painting, and lit a cigarette. 'Whisky and beer,' he grunted. He squinted through the smoke at the bar menu. 'And something to eat,' he added, pointing to some pies.

He propped his painting against the bar.

A man in a postman's hat was leaning there. 'No sky in it,' he said, pointing to the empty space above the church spire, the lights in the village houses and the distant hills.

'No, not yet,' grunted Vincent, wolfing the pie.

'Don't I know you?' said the postman, draining his pint glass. 'I remember now. That's it, you're that preacher fellow. You read from the gospels during the strikes to try and calm things down.'

Vincent recalled the downtrodden faces of the miners. His heart had bled for them when the violence began. Finally, even they had been forced to abandon him. That was when he'd first really started to paint. His bleak canvases provided a release from his despair: a stepping stone. Vincent gulped down another whisky and a beer.

The music was coming to an end. Vincent rummaged in his rucksack and found a worn Bible – a present from his father, a minister of religion. He stumbled onto the small stage.

Immediately he was back in the chapel with his brother Theo – dear, loyal Theo – listening to their father. The flat noses, thick lips and coarse hair of the members of the congregation revealed where and how they lived, betrayed their backbreaking toil in the fields around the village. The clouds passed over the chapel: sunlight flooded the small window, shone on the rich, grainy, polished pews, on the fair hair and faded print dresses of the Van Else susters, who did not smile when Vincent turned to admire them.

He began to read:

How blest are those who know that they are poor:
The kingdom of Heaven is theirs.
How blest are the sorrowful:
They shall find consolation.

In the silence that followed, a profound melancholy seemed to fill the bar.

The bell rang for last orders. The lights dimmed.

'Don't stop,' a voice taunted him. Vincent looked up. It was Garrigan, Christine at his side. Vincent's anger returned, his longing for a selfless love. He reached into his rucksack for his palette knife and lunged at his rival.

*   *   *   *

Vincent looked up at the starry night sky and applied two or three rapid brush strokes, standing back to examine the whirling pools of colour. His stars were no mere pinpricks of distant light but vast vibrant swirls of exploding turbulence.

A man stood next to him, holding an electric lamp. 'Time to go in now,' said Vincent's companion, sensing that the sky was finished at last. Complete, the crowded canvas spoke to him, comforted him in some strange way. Small as he was, it made him feel part of one single huge creation, world upon world.

The two men folded the easel, gathered up brushes and paints, and returned once more to the harsh light of a small upstairs room in the south wing.

A BRIDE IN THE HAND

I'd already seen Patricia Armstrong hovering, wicker basket in hand, by the supermarket entrance, and then again as she walked serenely up and down the aisles like a general inspecting troops on parade.

Halfway down one aisle she turned unexpectedly and bumped into me.

'Are you still working?' she asked, head on, no hesitation.

'Well, yes, no – I was made redundant last week,' I stammered, trying not to meet her gaze. Patrica had once been a shapely woman, but her hips had thickened and a slight stoop made her seem smaller. Her hands had aged, but her nails were finely shaped – polished and painted in a neutral shade. Her long fingers displayed twenty-five years' worth of diamond rings, glittering like needles of frost under moonlight. Her fair hair was thinner, highlighted, floating around her shoulders just as it used to do in her younger days. Her tweed costume was well cut, and her voice came in breathy, husky bursts, like the waves of perfume from the freesias on the flower display close by.

'Roger still works four days a week,' said Patricia. 'We've got a wedding to pay for in September. It's Jane. Yes, I knew you'd be surprised.'

I nodded – she seemed to have the things she wanted to say stacked up in her mind like records in a jukebox. She'd been holding her sunglasses folded in her hand but now she perched them on her forehead.

'I suppose the wedding will be at St Helen's.' I was flustered, struggling for something to say.

Close by, two supermarket trolleys locked wheels, full to overflowing. Over the public address system, a flat, nasal voice announced special offers on the delicatessen counter. Patricia placed a small sprig of broccoli into her wire basket. She won't take part in that scramble, I thought.

'Not at St Helen's, no – not there. St Helen's only has one bell but Wood Enderby has six. Besides, all my family connections are there.'

I nodded – I'd no chance now of bagging any of the special offers at the delicatessen.

'They met at Cambridge. They both got firsts in physics and now they're both chartered accountants. Jane's with Ernst Whinney and her fiancé is with Price Waterhouse.'

An alliance of accountancy royalty, then.

'It'll just be a small family wedding at Rudley Grange. A marquee with windows, and round tables – so much better for conversation, don't you think?'

I imagined sunset at Rudley Grange, grand and melancholy, soft light shining on its lake and elegant fountain.

'We like him. They look so happy together. His name's Harley-Payne.'

'Harley and Jane. The names sound really good together,' I said politely. Well, I had to try and make some contribution to the conversation.

'No, no, it's Peter and Jane. Harley-Payne is their surname – it's hyphenated, you know. Peter's family have homes in Northumberland and Berkshire. Oh! I nearly forgot to say. His uncle is an Air Vice-Marshal. He'll be at the wedding too, and in uniform possibly. There are bound to be photographs in *The Journal*.'

And then she remembered her manners. 'How are your family?' she asked.

'Jack's in Liverpool and Alan's in Stoke-on-Trent,' I replied but, as I paused for breath she broke in again.

'James is in Detroit. He's coming over for his sister's wedding, then he's flying on to Hong Kong for a conference. He was head-hunted by the Americans. His research has been published in *The Lancet*. I'm so proud of him and so is his father. James finds the Americans so friendly. We've already been for a fitting for the dress.'

Patricia reached for a small packet of tissues and added them to the sprig of broccoli. 'Peter's an Old Haymerian. He's going on a rugby tour to Samoa and New Zealand before the wedding.'

*   *   *   *

It was several weeks later before I saw Patricia Armstrong again. This time I walked straight over to her. I knew I'd be bumping into her sooner or later. Get it over with now, I thought to myself. Anyway, I like to hear about family news – especially happy occasions like weddings. I'd try and share in her joy – hopefully just for a short time.

'Peter met a New Zealand girl while he was in Samoa and never came home.' Face pale, Patricia blurted out the news. Her intense blue eyes clouded with tears.

'Oh dear,' I said sympathetically. The fracture that had suddenly disrupted her planned and orderly life was apparent for all to see. The chance to luxuriate in the final preparations for the wedding, as well as the day itself, had been denied her.

'So the wedding never took place?' I continued helplessly.

'That's right,' she snapped, dabbing her puffy eyes with a small tissue. 'I'm not sleeping at all.'

I could see her bedside table: the glass of water, the sleeping tablets, the luminous face of her little bedside clock turning slowly to morning after a fitful night's sleep.

'Perhaps it was a passing infatuation,' I said, transporting myself, in imagination at least, from the overcast Yorkshire day to the sensuous beauty of Samoa. Well, I'd been young once.

I leaned forward. I didn't like to see her tearful. 'Look, let me take you for a coffee or something. I usually go to the chapel just around the corner.'

After we'd finished our coffees, she picked up a leaflet from the display in the entrance hall. It showed the face of a child in a headscarf.

'I vaguely remember this,' said Patricia. 'What happened exactly?'

I paused before returning the crockery to the serving counter. 'It was an experiment at the Chernobyl Nuclear Plant in the Ukraine, in 1986. The whole thing went disastrously wrong and one of the reactors exploded. Afterwards there was a rise in the number of thyroid cancer cases, and many more babies were born with disabilities. Some parents just couldn't cope and abandoned their children altogether.'

Together we looked at a calendar with more photographs of the Chernobyl children.

'How dreadful,' she murmured.

'A network of people in this country, including some from this chapel, bring the children over for holidays. It boosts their battered immune systems and increases their life expectancy.'

'That's very kind,' said Patricia. 'I didn't realise. Have you ever seen any of these children?'

'Yes, I once spotted a group arriving at the airport. They looked like little scarecrows. Some were holding their trousers up with string and carrying their belongings in plastic bags.'

Now it was my turn to feel emotional.

'Thanks for bringing me here,' said Patricia, as I helped her into her coat. 'I feel a bit better. Can I leave something for their next visit?' She hesitated. 'There's something I haven't told you as well. It's Jane. She's expecting Peter's baby.'

Patricia bought a calendar and leafed through it again, intent on the faces of the Chernobyl children. Her thoughts, I imagine, were no longer on Wood Enderby and its six bells, but on a christening in the village church.

BEYOND THE PALE

Below decks in the crowded third-class compartment of a British steamship crossing the North Sea, groups of shabbily dressed passengers lolled or stretched out on the floor in the early morning half-light. Among them were a group all fleeing the same Russian village: Isaac Sadosky, the shoemaker; Sol Cohen, the tailor; Woolf Kossoff, the cabinet-maker; Abraham Bloom, the hawker, with a pile of hats on his head; and lastly Menachem Kurek, the carpenter.

On the hard bench they'd shared since leaving Rotterdam sat Menachem's wife Miriam, grey and haggard from years of poverty and the hardships of the journey. Asleep in a wooden cradle carved by Menachem lay a baby girl, Magdalena, the child of Miriam's dead sister. The Kureks' two daughters, Maria and Elizabeth, and son, Tamar – all pale but for dark patches under their eyes – were awake and sat solemnly at the other side of their mother. Meanwhile Menachem's brother Benjamin snored rhythmically, his arm around his old Singer sewing machine.

Miriam tore off three pieces of onion bread – a gift from a dying Jewish woman on the ship. At home they might have been breakfasting on the remains of a herring, washed down by hot water, perhaps with a little sugar. A Polish tramp steamer, normally used for carrying livestock, had taken them as far as Lübeck in Germany, where they'd caught a labouring steam train to Rotterdam. Billowing black smoke has been our companion throughout this journey, mused Menachem – first from the train, now from the ship.

It was the Eve of the Sabbath, and Menachem felt hungry and grimy after two days at sea. How he longed to be in the bathhouse his cousin Simcha had described: Schewzik's Vapour Baths in Brick Lane supposedly offered the best massage in London.

This was the Kureks' second attempt to escape the Pale of Settlement since Tsar Alexander's assassination. The first time, the police had pounced and confiscated the family's costly official passport just as they were about to leave Riga. A few weeks later Menachem had bribed his way to a second passport shared with three others: Shoshana, a tall, dark-eyed girl from their own village; Leonard Slatkin, emotional and clown faced, whose violin playing had kept the children amused on the journey; and a secretive, bullet-headed man known only as Kever.

Sighing deeply, Menachem once again unfolded the crumpled letter bearing Simcha's address: 41 Pelham Street, Spitalfields – in London's East End. He glanced fondly at his son. Tamar could only speak two words of English: 'England' and 'London.' That's where they would celebrate his son's bar mitzvah. Perhaps Simcha would be able to provide honey cake and vodka and a small gift for the boy.

Shoshana was beginning to wake – stretching and shaking out her shoulder-length, blue-black hair. She smiled shyly at Menachem.

'Watch over my Shoshana until my nephew Abelov meets her on the quayside,' Gershon Klemantowski had instructed Menachem. The innkeeper had grown more emotional in his old age, and tears came quickly to his blood-shot eyes. Shoshana had been born to his second wife, when Gershon was in his fifties.

Shoshana had pleaded with her father to join her in a new life in England.
'I'm too old,' said Gershon, holding up his red, calloused hands as if making an offering in the synagogue. 'I have to stay, even though our people are penned more closely than ever in this godforsaken hell-hole. You're young. You're clever. You must leave for a better life in London. You know what happened to your cousin Nina when she got mixed up in politics.'

On their final Sabbath in the old country, the two families had celebrated with meat, unusual for them, noodle soup and a bottle of Gershon's vodka.

Menachem had done his best to reassure his old friend: 'The hand of God will care for Shoshana.' But who would care for Gershon? Without his daughter, the innkeeper would surely drift rudderless and seek even greater consolation in drink.

*   *   *   *

Morris Stein was lurking in a gin-shop on the quayside in Wapping, his doleful Jewish eyes racing over the crowds stepping off the steamships. Boat after boat had landed with the morning tide. Finally his eyes alighted on a young woman with long, blue-black hair. Good, he thought. This one's alone.

Morris stubbed out his thick cigar, drained his glass and picked up his cane. The same deception had worked many, many times.

People thronged the quayside, separating Shoshana from the Kureks. Deep, excitable Yiddish voices sounded above the English. Men with metal hand-trolleys loaded with bags weaved and bumped amongst the crowds. Horns blasted. Tall warehouses lined the docks, and nets full of cargo swung high above the scene before dropping like stones onto the crowded quay.

Simcha was there as promised to greet them.

'What did the Medical Officer have to say about Maria and Elizabeth?' asked Menachem.

His cousin stroked his stubbly grey beard: 'That they look a bit pale and need some fresh air. That's all. Don't worry.'

Menachem closed his eyes and offered a prayer of thanks, relieved that his family had finally reached their destination. Then he remembered his promise to Gershon – but he'd lost sight of Shoshana.

Further down the quay Morris Stein was about to approach her.

Stein always followed the same routine: a pause, a warm smile and a look of semi-recognition.

'Cousin Abelov?' asked Shoshana.

Stein's smiled grew broader. That was exactly what he wanted to hear.

'Abelov. Yes, I'm Cousin Abelov.' He placed a welcoming hand on the girl's shoulder. 'Quickly, come this way. Everything is arranged. Follow me and we'll have fewer problems with the authorities.'

The bullet-headed Kever – the third name on Menachem Kurek's passport – was watching closely. He had been hoping to meet up with men like Morris Stein.

Suddenly a hand reached out and gripped Stein by the arm. It was Abraham Hollander, a retired Jewish boxer, bearing the badge of the Hebrew Ladies' Protection Society.

Stein released Shoshana and handed her bags over to Hollander. 'There's a temporary shelter where you can stay until we find your relatives,' said the ex-boxer. He pointed to the man fast disappearing into the crowds. 'That Morris Stein is nothing but a common criminal.'

After all the hardships of the journey, Shoshana had been just a few steps from the misery of an East End brothel.

*   *   *   *

Meanwhile the sound of a piano had drawn Leonard Slatkin into a public house. During a short interval, Leonard summoned up all his courage, walked over to the instrument, lifted its lid, trailed his hand over the keys, sat down and started to play. He learned tunes by ear but he played like a professional: all his four brothers were musical. He finished by turning to his violin and playing a gypsy tune, haunting but lively. The applause was loud. Leonard Slatkin was Jewish and spoke no English – but no one minded that. Within an hour of landing on the Wapping quayside, Leonard Slatkin had found work.

*   *   *   *

'The winds and smoke blow mainly from the west of the city,' said Simcha. 'That's where the rich people live. There are many fine houses and parks. But we make plenty of smoke in the East End as well.'

He smiled at Menachem. The new immigrants picked up their few bags and took a final look downstream before trudging away from the broad sweep of the Thames. Wooden stanchions supporting the skeleton of a large ship loomed eerily through the fog.

'A battleship nearing completion,' said Simcha. 'The British navy is the most powerful in the world, you know.'

Menachem nodded. Then came a thunderous boom.

'What's that?' asked young Tamar, jamming his hands over his ears.

'It's the steam hammer at the Thames Ironworks,' replied Simcha. 'You can hear it for miles around.'

The fog had thickened in the late afternoon dusk, filling the streets and alleyways, blurring the outlines of terraced houses and tenement blocks. The family occasionally found itself dwarfed by massive, gloomy churches with blackened spires.

Wide eyed, Maria and Elizabeth coughed and shivered and clung to their mother's skirt. Uncle Benjamin hunched his shoulders and gasped for breath; Menachem carried the sewing-machine.

The Kureks walked wearily through the damp streets – the short, energetic Simcha leading the way. From time to time, crowds of workers with strange voices and heavy boots would burst out into the street, only to fade quickly into the gloom. Every step brought a new smell: glue, soap, rubber, tar. Eyes smarted, throats grew dry, voices cracked. High windows were lit abruptly by the glow of a furnace. Horses and carts clattered by.

In one doorway, Tamar tripped over a pile of rags: it was an old tramp, clutching a bottle. The boy peered through the door. Blanket-draped bodies lay listlessly on beds crammed together in a long, dark room.

'This is a night shelter,' said Simcha. 'Many folk are destitute in the East End. There's even a Jewish home for the elderly and infirm in Spitalfields. You can't get away from poverty, disease and hunger in this city – like the bad

59

weather.'

Simcha hurried them along. Menachem was clearly tired, disappointed in his new surroundings. 'Don't worry,' he continued. 'Everything's strange and you're all exhausted. Things will look different in the morning. Think of Mother Russia. She's not that maternal: summers, short and plagued with mosquitoes from the birch forests; winters, long, dark and bitingly cold; spring, with roads and fields waterlogged, rutted and muddy from the melting snow.'

'And our people oppressed by the authorities at every turn,' added Benjamin.

Behind a brightly lit shop window, a butcher – with bushy moustache, white apron, and a white shirt with the sleeves turned back – was serving beefsteak puddings. Simcha pointed to the sign above the window: 'Beef, pork and lard, it says.'

Miriam was shocked. 'They're open on the Eve of the Sabbath.'

'Yes, English shops don't close. There are many kosher butchers in Spitalfields though, supplied by a herd of cows just off the Whitechapel Road. And plenty of bagel bakeries.'

Two heavy horses emerged from an archway, startling the family. Snorting, steaming, harness rattling, their feathery covered hooves struck the cobbled streets like hammers on an anvil.

The Kureks breathed in the sweet, aromatic aroma of hops.

'That's a brewery,' said Simcha. 'Londoners like their beer. There's a tannery further down the street, though.'

Tamar covered his mouth and nose.

Coal fires blazed in the public houses. Workers were drinking beer. They don't look hostile, thought Menachem. They all seem at ease.

'English people like sport, you know,' said Simcha. 'Tamar must learn to play cricket in the street with the other children. And there's a Jewish Boys' Club on Brick Lane that goes camping in summer.'

The fog hung heavy in the air as the last watery light of day drained quickly from the sky.

'We must hurry,' said Simcha. 'These streets aren't safe after dark. There are gangs round here.'

They turned a corner in the gathering dusk: yellow candlelight was visible, first in one window and then in all the front parlours in the long street of shabby terraced houses.

'Mazeltov,' said Simcha.

'Mazeltov,' replied Menachem, embracing his cousin, kissing his wife and placing his arms around his children.

Jewish shops lined the streets. All the signs were in Yiddish, so too the torn newspaper placard flapping in the light wind. The smells were familiar. Small grocery shops sold pickled herring and cucumbers, smoked salmon and onion bread. A butcher's shop advertised salt beef.

'There are many Jews in London now, nearly all here in the East End,' said Simcha. 'We've at least fifteen synagogues within walking distance. Some in attics and back rooms. There's even a Jewish cemetery in Whitechapel.'

Suddenly a door swung open onto a small, dark room. Gathered protectively around a huge pile of potatoes, a man, his wife and their five dark-eyed children stared at them suspiciously.

'A potato seller and his family,' said Simcha, grinning. 'There are many different trades around here, though most men are tailors and work from home.' Simcha ran his hand over Tamar's threadbare coat. 'In a few days a new suit for the boy perhaps – for his bar mitzvah.'

For the first time since they left Wapping, it was quiet here, peaceful: no shoppers or workers thronging the streets; no excited Yiddish cries echoing in the alleyways; no strange English voices filling the air.

In Spitalfields, on this Eve of the Sabbath, all work had ceased. In one window, candlelight outlined a man in a yarmulke, goblet in hand: he was leading the Kiddush and sanctifying the bread and wine.

It could have been a fragment of their old home torn out and dropped amidst the new.

They entered Simcha's terraced house. Proudly he showed them his tailor's workshop in the attic, with its four Singer sewing-machines, a tailoring table, a finishing table, and one for pressing. Wool particles floated in air heavy with the strong smell of dyes.

Benjamin nodded approvingly to Simcha: he'd be able to work here. He coughed and placed his hand on his back as a renewed spasm of pain crossed his face.

My brother will not make many suits to hang in London homes, thought Menachem – but for the children, our children, life will be infinitely richer. The girls would lose that solemn look. Tamar was clever with his hands. He'd become an architect – not a carpenter like his father.

The Kureks had arrived in London at last. Tomorrow, on the Sabbath, they would go to the synagogue and offer special thanks and prayers.

THE FAIR

Twice a year the fair arrived like an invading army – its trucks, fume-filled generators and flamboyant caravans camping on a piece of unloved derelict land that lay around a long-abandoned corner shop. For the railway passengers on the viaduct above the small town, it was a cluster of coloured lights glowing far below among the long lines of squat terraced houses.

'The fair's back,' said Jenny Marston. Her grandma was in hospital and Jenny had heard the hammering and shouting as she returned from her daily visit.

Deep in his armchair, Ken Marston nodded and yawned. Like most of his overweight, baggy-eyed drinking friends in the Spread Eagle, her father had a long-term medical condition and no longer worked.

'It opens this evening,' she continued.

Sylvia Marston was applying mascara, getting ready for a late shift at the biscuit factory where she worked as a supervisor. 'How's Gran?' she asked.

'About the same,' replied Jenny. 'They've moved her to another part of the ward.' She didn't like to say it was a side room.

Sylvia glanced in the mirror and smoothed on her lipstick with her little finger. 'I'm going to be late,' she said.

On the small black-and-white TV screen in the corner, a bloated figure in dark glasses and a tasselled one-piece suit stumbled on stage, singing soulfully that love was tender and sweet.

'He's going downhill even faster than me,' said Ken, standing up to sharpen his cut-throat razor on the taut strap fastened to a hook on the wall.

Sylvia shouted to her daughter: 'Put the light on, Jenny, before he cuts himself to shreds. I don't want to be the one rushing him to casualty.'

Ken's razor was a constant cause of tension in the house. Sylvia was always pleading with him to get a safety razor or even an electric shaver. 'Don't talk to your father when he's shaving' had been her mother's refrain throughout Jenny's childhood.

'Ouch,' yelled Ken as he nicked his chin. The music on the television had set him thinking about Doris Day. Now she was lovely. She was radiant, happy, voice of silk – not moody and miserable like the figure on the screen. Humming 'Secret Love', Ken stuck a piece of toilet-paper over a nick on his fleshy red face and happily contemplated another long night in the Spread Eagle.

'I'll take my curlers out at work,' said Sylvia, patting her hair and hitching up her skirt. 'That'll have to do for now.'

She glanced at the clock, covering her hair with the red chiffon scarf that matched her shoes. A half-smoked cigarette smouldered in the stained groove of the glass ashtray. 'If you do go out, don't be late,' she shouted to Jenny.

'Same for you too,' she rushed on, turning to Ken. 'Don't wait up for me. There's some of yesterday's pie left over for tea and I'll be getting a lift home.'

Ken watched her go, running his fingers thoughtfully over the nick on his chin. He'd have something to eat in the Eagle as usual: Sylvia's dried-up pie was fit only for the swans on the canal.

*   *   *   *

Up in the attic, Jenny had closed her bedroom door, trying to block out the image of the faltering figure on the TV screen. She lay on her bed, listened to his voice from the fairground, looked up at his face on the ceiling, the walls, and her LP sleeves. In her imagination, she was standing on the thickly carpeted corridor of the cinema in town. Beyond the velvety, brass-studded, padded door, he'd be riding a tractor, disappearing into the sunset, shirt-sleeves rolled up over tightly bulging biceps; he'd be frolicking in the foaming surf, his dark mane wet, no longer slicked back with grease or sweat; he'd be wearing his army uniform, saluting deferentially, smiling at virginal, compliant girls in freshly ironed skirts that fanned out like his long fingers across the strings of his guitar.

Another of his songs drifted in from the fair and Jenny got dressed to go out.

The night air was pungent with a mixture of brandy snaps, diesel and onions as Jenny approached the fair. Under the coloured lights, yellow smoke rose from a noisy, vibrating generator. The youth collecting money on the waltzer had a curl to his lip, a soulful look in his dark eyes, and a black, greasy quiff that rose and fell like the floor beneath him. Weaving among the carriages, his worn leather money-pouch hanging from his skinny waist, he rested his hand on Jenny's bare shoulder and she felt a rush of excitement. With a little backwards hop he returned to the centre of the ride, a few lank strands of hair flopping over one eye.

Galloping nowhere, going faster and faster, the lights melted into one dizzy blur for Jenny. The youth came and sat next to her and for a time they were alone in the carriage, the safety rail hard against her thrumming heart. He held a coke bottle to his lips and with a shrug offered Jenny a drink. Her eyes shone like the stars scattered in the heavens above.

* * * *

Solemn faces greeted Jenny when she arrived home. 'Is something the matter?' she asked.

'Yes, love,' replied Sylvia, eyes filling with tears. 'It's your gran. She died this evening. We didn't know where you were.'

Jenny placed her arm around her mother. 'I stayed late at the fair.' The music coming from the fair was faint, distant and sleepy: subdued like the Marston family.

'Cause of death tranquillisers and barbiturates,' said Ken, turning off the TV.

Jenny was puzzled. 'Grandma?' she asked.

'No, that rock 'n roll fella who shakes his hips,' Ken replied innocently. 'Elvis Presley. It's just been on the news.'

'Died?' wailed Jenny, tears springing to her eyes. 'Died? No, he can't have.' She rushed upstairs, threw herself onto her bed and sobbed as though her heart would break. Her damp hands clawed at his pictures, clutched at her sheet. How would she make it through the night?

Hearing her cry, Ken got up to go to his daughter.

'No leave her, love,' said Sylvia. 'Stay here. We've things to do.'

Unable to sleep, Jenny got up and dressed. She pulled open the top drawer of her bedside cabinet and removed a medallion containing his picture. She looked at it for a few moments, running the silver chain through her fingers like a rosary. Then mechanically she placed it in her pocket.

She set off for the fair, stopping on the way to stare into the stagnant water of the canal. She felt for the medallion and took it from her pocket. Behind her a dog whined in one of the caravans. A light came on and shone through the small window with its lacy net curtains. The door opened and a shaft of light streamed onto the damp earth. He walked towards her and again placed his hand on her shoulder. He didn't see her discard the medallion. It fell to earth like a fallen glove and remained there long after the fair had left town.

THEY MATTER

Only the old metal street sign remains. When the houses in this street and its neighbour were levelled for parking space in the 1960s, the Victorian sign survived on the wall of this corner fish and chip shop, where it still hangs today with the help of two metal pins.

A young girl with painted fingernails, ear-studs and nose-studs serves my fish and chips. Tufts of hair stick through the gaps in her baseball hat. 'See you again,' she manages to say as she hands me my change. I remember a previous owner who served in a starched white overall and wore his white hat at a jaunty angle. His movements were quick and businesslike, and he was full of lively chatter as he lowered fish into hissing pans of fat.

My mother used to skip down this street when it was a long terrace of houses. Shortly afterwards she was doing two cleaning jobs every day. Buckets of coal had to be carried to third-floor attics, grates cleared of cinders and fires lit. A shop stood a few doors down from 27 Stanley Street, the two-bedroomed family home. My mother worked there too. One minute she'd be selling bags of coal, she told me, the next bread.

It's a dark, overcast November day with occasional needles of hail. Pools of yesterday's rain mark what I think is the site of my grandparents' house. I stare at my unfocused reflection in the murky, shimmering water and imagine their faces. Uncomplicated memories of childhood return to me. A short, gloomy passageway led from the front door. On the wall hung a large head-and-shoulders photograph of Grandfather Tom from his playing days with Goole RUFC. He wears a small cap with a tassel on the top. The front room was largely unused and sparsely furnished: it was cold, north facing and mausoleum like. The back room, brightened only feebly by light from a single gas mantle, was the main living area, its slab of a stone sink standing like an altar in front of the net-curtained sash window. The fire heated an oven from behind whose heavy door came savoury cooking smells. What I remember most of all was the heady, rich aroma of twist tobacco from Grandfather Tom's pipe, and the kindly, expressive eyes my mother inherited from him. A thick cloth, tasselled like a blanket, covered the table. There were a handful of ornaments – faded and veined with age. I took a childlike comfort from the sense of contentment in this room – a feeling I've never quite experienced anywhere else.

Grandfather Tom came to stay with us once, shortly after he was widowed. A tall figure framed in our doorway, he looked a little neglected, frail and worn out. His suit was crumpled and his scarf was tied carelessly round his neck, but this retired, rugby-playing shipyard riveter still showed signs of the strong man he had been in his prime.

Grandmother's forenames were Mary Ann Ruth, but she was always known as Polly. In her long, shiny, black dress, she resembled Queen Victoria in mourning for Prince Albert; she spoke very little and always seemed to be in the background preparing a meal. I only saw her a few times so my memories of her are fragmentary. It seems to me now that the turn of the twentieth century and the 1950s somehow sat side by side in this room. Grandfather's final message to her in the newspaper clipping enclosed in the family bible was touching in its simplicity: God bless you, dear heart, till we meet again.

She spent all her married life in this terraced, two-bedroomed house and gave birth to ten children between 1904 and 1928. For five years, her mother, the daughter of a Suffolk master mariner, lived in that mausoleum of a front room. Most unpopular with my grandfather, so my mother told me.

Polly's seven sons always worked and never seemed to be any trouble: some had two jobs. John, her favourite, sang solo in the parish church and died aged just twenty-two as a soldier in Malaya. I have one of his letters, full of life, written only a few days before his death. Herbert, as a sergeant in the army, saw military action in Italy during the Second World War. Joe, who worked on the docks, fell into a ship's hold and was never quite the same again. Another brother, Horace, suffered from fits and died as a child, while Harry, a quiet and withdrawn bachelor, was much loved by my mother and died in his early fifties. Ted, the most handsome, had shown much promise, but was married while young to a much older, twice-widowed lady, who was known to be a little bit volatile. My one memory of Tommy was that he told me to rub spit into my hair instead of using hair-cream.

There were three daughters: Doris, the eldest, uncomplicated, placid and seemingly never envious of others; Mary, full of quick-witted humour, amusing everyone she met on buses or in shops; and Edna, my mother – gentle, cheerful and selfless all her life. I remember a letter to me that reflected her loving nature, found by chance in a teapot by my daughter, Elizabeth, on the day of my mother's funeral.

I move on from the site of 27 Stanley Street and glance back at the blackened tower and spire of the parish church, with its flying buttresses and slender refurbished pinnacles. Apart from the graceful spire, the remainder of this grey and solid-looking Victorian church somehow doesn't please my eye or raise my spirits. It still dominates this inland port just as it did when my parents lived there, and they must have glanced up at it many times, as I do now. Today it stands shoulder to shoulder with cranes and grain silos.

Fragments of my parents' lives surface randomly: the 'demob' telegram from King's Cross in 1945; the torn newspaper clipping of their wedding; two faded, pressed carnation sprays in a Bible; the honeymoon journey by steam train to Blackpool; and a photograph of the two of them strolling along the sea-front looking happy and relaxed. I remember my parents' simple ways, gentle humility and, in this age of shopping, complete lack of acquisitive instincts.

The Burlington Hotel on Alexandra Street stands close by. This is where my 41-year-old father met my 24-year-old mother, who worked there before their marriage, when it was a hotel as well as a public house. Through those same swing doors my father would have entered in his sailor suit, his enormous canvas kitbag on his shoulder. By this time he'd spent a full thirty years in the Royal Navy, having joined at sixteen as a 'Ganges boy,' when life in this naval training establishment on the Suffolk coast was austere, demanding and often brutal. He must have climbed the infamous dry-land Shotley Mast, and I regret that he never discussed this experience with me. In December 1914, six months after leaving HMS Ganges at the age of seventeen, he was serving on HMS Cornwall, taking part in the battle of the Falkland

Tom Marritt, retired shipyard riveter.

Islands and receiving a bounty for the enemy ship they destroyed. He also went on to serve in the Second World War.

Once a handsome three-storey Victorian building, the Burlington now looks shabby. I look briefly through a window where two young men are engrossed in a game of pool. I remember crowds of flat-capped working men behind a haze of pipe and cigarette smoke at the town's football ground in the 1950s. Grandfather always made sure we sat near the touchline so we could see. He liked sport. An old photograph in the Goole Times shows him in his rugby kit outside the Buchanan Hotel in 1902, when he was vice-captain of the town's team. He always cultivated two allotments – a necessity with a large family to feed – and continued to do so to the end of his life. His allotment shed always smelled of twine, my cousin tells me. He also liked literature and crosswords. I picture him, puffing away at his pipe and reading under the soft glow of that hissing gas mantle in his uncomfortable steel-rimmed spectacles.

From the Burlington I walk a short distance to another long street of terraced houses. I stop outside 36 Phoenix Street, where my father, also called George Sweeting, lived for a short time with his mother, sister and stepfather in the early 1900s. At the far end of this street is a high brick wall, once part of the Phoenix Iron Foundry. My paternal grandmother died at this address in 1912, when she was only thirty-five. Somehow an impression of sadness lingers around her short life. She was born in the local workhouse and it seems that her own mother largely abandoned her. Did her early life cause her to become wilful and headstrong, or bitter and subdued? I'll never know, and my father never said much when I asked him about her. Shortly after her death, and with some encouragement from the local vicar, my father joined the Royal Navy.

I've made my way to the high riverbank now. The open sky, the flat landscape and the broad sweep of the River Ouse is a change, and a comforting presence after the gloomy back streets of terraced houses. I look down on large, three-storey Victorian houses, built like fortresses, with tall chimney stacks and stone-mullioned windows. In times past, I suppose, the inland port's doctors and sea captains would have lived here.

The river has big loops and bends. Eddying currents create a scene of alternate calm and movement. Steam is intermittently released from the direction of the docks, and the sounds of chains sliding across a floor drown out the gentle lapping of the water. Little plumes of smoke rise from distant chimneys. On the opposite bank, birds have settled in a curving line on the mudflats. There are no boats on the river today. I'm alone except for a solitary woman walking her dog. Where I'm standing now, townsfolk once promenaded in days gone by, waiting for a flotilla of boats to come in on the tide: a regular steam ferry service covered the network of rivers for miles around. In the days of sail, schooners, ketches and keels, full riggers, barques and barquentines all sailed into the docks, loading and unloading their various cargoes. A giant anchor, a memorial to all who sailed from the port, stands on the riverbank.

Orange and white street lamps glow in the last of the light now draining from the sky. It has started to rain and high on the riverbank I feel a chill wind. I turn up my collar and make my way back to my car, parked close to where I believe my mother was born. Through the rain-splattered windscreen, a nearby streetlight illuminates the Stanley Street sign, still hanging by its two metal pins.